BRIDGET'S BEAU

River's End Ranch Book 11

KIRSTEN OSBOURNE

Unlimited Dreams

Bridget's Beau
Book Eleven in River's End Ranch
Kirsten Osbourne
Cover art by Erin Dameron-Hill

Introduction

Bridget Taylor was excited to be on a trip to Idaho for her twin sister's wedding. While they didn't always get along when they were together, they missed each other terribly when they were apart. Soon after her arrival, her sister Kaya introduced her to a man she thought she'd be compatible with, but the twinkle in Kaya's eye worried Bridget. Exactly who was she setting her up with? When she saw the man for the first time, her heart caught in her throat, sinking just as quickly when she realized his profession.

Kevin Roberts had known for years that he would end up being a pastor. When he found out River's End Ranch, a beautiful destination ranch in Northern Idaho, was hiring a pastor, he couldn't pass up the job. After his first couple of months on the ranch a buddy's wife introduced him to her sister, and knew immediately the sister had to be his wife. But what were her hang ups with him being a pastor? And could he convince her that marrying him was the right thing for both of them?

To sign up for Kirsten Osbourne's mailing list text 'Bob" to 42828

Acknowledgments

I'm dedicating this book to two people, my mother, Vicki Hamielec, and my sister, Brenda Mich. I think we can all agree that this book wouldn't have happened without the two of them. We all went on a cruise together over the summer, and Brenda and I spent a great deal of time stabbing each other with shrimp forks and posing with the different photographers. We amused ourselves in a happy non-destructive way. Less than a month later, I found out Mom had made Brenda sandwiches shaped like butterflies that she found when she opened her lunch box in the nurse's break room at work. Brenda wasn't nearly as amused as Mom and I were…

Chapter One

BRIDGET TAYLOR SAT QUIETLY WAITING for her plane to taxi to the gate in Lewiston, Idaho. Both of her parents were beside her, and they were all seeing her twin, Kaya, for the first time in a couple of months. None of them had met Kaya's new husband, Glen, yet but they'd heard so much about him, it was as if they'd known him for years.

As soon as they were at the gate, Bridget, who was on the aisle, sprang to her feet to pull down all the carry-ons she and her parents had put in the overhead bin, while her mother got slowly to her feet. "I think airplane seats get smaller every time I fly!" her mother complained.

Bridget almost said, "Maybe you get bigger," but she thought better of it. She was going to control her tongue and have a nice trip if it killed her. "Kaya said she got us a cabin at the River's End Ranch, where Glen works, and there will be a car here to pick us up."

"Sending a car to pick us up like she's too important to come herself!" Dad shook his head. "What is the world coming to when you can't pick up your parents from the airport for your own wedding reception?"

"I'm sure she had reasons, Dad." Bridget threw her bag over her shoulder and waited in the long line to get off the plane. She wouldn't admit it out loud, but she'd actually missed her sister. When they were together, they tended to fight, unless they were involved in some sort of *shenanigans*, but that didn't mean they didn't love each other. Why, Bridget had even bought a new set of shrimp forks for each of them before she'd gotten on the plane. How could a sister not love a new set of shrimp forks?

"You're going to be on your best behavior," her mother hissed in her ear. "Do you hear me, Bridget Elaine?"

Bridget wrinkled her nose. "How come I got stuck with Bridget Elaine and Kaya got Kaya Cheyenne? You love her more than me, don't you?" She carefully kept her back to her mother to hide her smirk as she heard her mother's sharp intake of breath.

"Don't you start with me! I had to get up at the butt crack of dawn to fly here for this reception, and I'm not in a good mood! Who has a reception so far from everyone they love? Only your sister!"

Bridget didn't bother to respond, recognizing the rant for what it was. Her mother was tired and sore after flying all day, and she was expressing her frustration with that by complaining about Kaya. Their mother loved them both desperately, but in their family, love was shown in a way that wouldn't be perfectly acceptable in a *normal* family.

They proceeded to baggage claim as soon as they made it off the plane, and Bridget finally breathed deeply for the first time in hours. The flight from DFW had seemed to take forever, and she was ready to be settled somewhere. Besides, the germs on planes were killers. Who wanted to think about that? Not her!

Bridget was a nurse for a small family practice in Denton, Texas. She'd started out working in nursing homes, but they just hadn't worked well for her, though her best friend, Jenni, was very happy in the nursing home where she'd worked since before graduation, first as a nurse's aid, and now as a full-fledged nurse.

Secretly, Bridget hoped that some of her sister's luck would rub off on her, and there would be a handsome, intelligent man waiting to take them to the ranch. They would fall in love on the way there, and spend the entire week in one another's company, completely unaware of anyone around them. At the end of the week, he would tell her he couldn't live without her, and she would only go back to Texas for long enough to pack up her apartment and work out a two weeks' notice. Then it would be back to Idaho, land of mountains and lakes and Bigfoot.

Bridget wasn't so sure about the Bigfoot thing, but Kaya had reassured her it was true. Of course she hadn't believed Kaya about anything since she had told her that all men named Matt were perfect for being romance heroes. Why Matt? Even Kaya didn't know.

At baggage claim, instead of a handsome man, they found Kaya, and Bridget hurried to her sister to hug her, while getting a shrimp fork out of her pocket and concealing it in her hand. Mid-hug, she stabbed her sister in the bottom with her shrimp fork, just as she felt her own stab on the shoulder.

The sisters looked at each other and laughed hysterically, grimacing as they saw the look their mother was giving them. "Where is he? I have to see this perfect man you married!" Bridget looked around for someone who looked like he was with Kaya.

Kaya made a face. "I never said he was perfect. Just that he's perfect for me. See the difference?" She brandished a shrimp fork warningly as she asked.

Bridget rolled her eyes, stepping away from her sister so her parents could hug her. "Is he here?"

Kaya shook her head. "Nope. He's at the ranch today. There was a big group wanting to go on a trail ride, and his boss needed another man. He was planning on coming until the very last minute."

Bridget was careful not to show her disappointment. She was very curious about her sister's new husband. "You actually drove? It's miraculous! So tell us about this cabin we're staying in!"

Kaya ignored her sister's comments about her driving. "I got you the Bearfoot Bungalow. You're going to love it. It overlocks the river, and it's just gorgeous. No one has said, but I'm pretty sure Kelsi named it. She's the Bigfoot hunter I told you about." Kaya hugged their mother, who was more Bridget's height than Kaya's.

Bridget the Midget is what Kaya liked to call her. Of course Kaya was of Amazonian proportions, and Bridget was compact-sized, so it made sense that Kaya would see her as a midget.

After their parents had hugged Kaya, Bridget linked her arm with her sister's. "Any eligible men on the ranch?"

Kaya grinned, a mischievous look coming into her eye. "I think you should meet Kevin. He's handsome, sweet, and very eligible."

"Kevin, huh? Tell me all about him!"

"I'll do better. I'll introduce you! He'll be at the reception."

"I can't wait to meet him! Is he a good friend of Glen's?"

Kaya bit her lip, seeming to hide a laugh. "They're not super close. He just moved to the ranch a short while ago, but he's a good guy."

"I'll look forward to it." Their dad gave Bridget her

suitcase, and she took it by the handle to pull it behind her. "So what is there to do on this ranch we're staying at? Anything fun?"

Kaya laughed softly. "There's something to do every day. There's an Old West town to explore, four-wheelers to ride around on, horses to ride, mountains to climb, rivers to raft, and so very much more. Seriously, you could move here and never leave the ranch." She frowned. "It's cooler now though, so no rivers to raft, and the pool is closed. Maybe we'll get some snow while you're here!"

"They're not hiring a nurse, are they?" Bridget asked. It sounded so amazing she never wanted to leave. And despite how she and her sister behaved at times, she would love to have her around. She'd missed her since she moved to Idaho.

"You know, I think they are. The old nurse, Emily, announced she was planning on retiring last week."

"Wait, why is there a nurse?"

Kaya glanced over her shoulder to ensure their parents were ready as she started toward the car. "There's a first aid station right there on the ranch. Mainly for minor stuff. If an injury is serious, they care flight the person here to Lewiston. I don't know how busy the nurse is kept, but it's nice to know there's one on the property. There are so many dangerous activities."

Bridget's mind was spinning. It wasn't where she'd seen herself when she'd decided to go to nursing school, but it seemed right. Very right. Maybe she'd talk to the ranch owners about it. "Tell me more about Kevin!"

Kaya laughed, shaking her head. "Just wait to meet him."

Once they were in the car, Bridget leaned back and closed her eyes. Their father had commandeered driving the thing, claiming that he'd never trusted Kaya's driving, which suited Kaya nicely. She hated driving, though Lewiston was not nearly as bad as Dallas traffic.

Kaya and Bridget both sat in the back, together. Neither of them were stabbing the other with their shrimp fork, but both had them at the ready. Why own a shrimp fork if you didn't use it to stab your sister?

* * *

"Wake up, Midget! We're at the ranch!" Kaya's voice was insistent.

Bridget thought about slapping her sister away, but instead she groaned and opened her eyes. She'd needed that short nap. Well, she'd needed a long nap, but there hadn't been time for that.

She peered out the window for the first time at a big sign that read, "River's End Ranch."

Kaya was practically bouncing with her excitement to show the place to her family. "The diner's over there. Kelsi runs the place, and she's pregnant. She's not showing much, but pretend she is. It'll make her day!"

Bridget nodded. She was all about making the natives happy. "You said a family owns this place?"

"Yes! There are six siblings. Four brothers and the two youngest are twin girls. They're identical, but they work hard to not look alike. You know what I mean."

Bridget knew *exactly* what her sister meant. When the two of them were little their mother had dressed them alike, even though they had truly never been similar. Kaya had always been tall and fair, and Bridget was petite with brunette hair. No, they hadn't favored at all, but still they'd dressed very differently in high school, not really even wanting people to know they were sisters, let alone twins.

Kaya gave directions to their father until he

parked in front of a cabin. Bridget bounced out of the car, glad she'd gotten her nap and thrilled to be there. "Is there a hot tub? I could use a hot tub about now!"

"There is! It's on the back porch. Come on, and I'll show you around. This is where Liz, May, and I stayed when I came here for the first time."

Twenty minutes later, Bridget was settled into a small bedroom with a private bath. She sighed contentedly. She was used to having an apartment to herself, but if she had to share quarters with her parents, this was how she wanted to do it.

She walked out into the living room, which was basically the same big room as the kitchen. It was a very open floor plan. "I approve of your choice, Kaya. You did something right."

"I do a lot of things right!" Kaya said, wrinkling her nose at her sister. "Don't make me stab you with a shrimp fork!"

"You may have fans who think you're something special, but I knew you before you were potty trained. Think about it!" Bridget walked into the living room to sit with her parents. "What are the plans now?"

"I'm going to fix dinner for all of us tonight. And to make numbers even, I texted Glen and asked that he invite Kevin to supper."

Bridget perked up at that. "Sounds good. Has he responded?"

"He said he'd be there." Kaya stood, rubbing the back of her neck. "I'm going to ride home with Glen. I'll draw you a map to get to our house, but really, it's just across the highway. Very easy."

"Write it down for me," their dad told her. "And are we going to meet this man you married before supper?"

Kaya nodded. "He's supposed to be here in about twenty minutes to take me home. You can meet him then."

Bridget was honestly thrilled for her sister. As much as they fought, there was no one she loved more. "How long were you on the ranch before you met Glen?"

"About fifteen minutes. We stopped at the diner before coming in to the cabin, and he was there getting his dinner. I took one look at him and knew I'd spend the rest of my life in love with him." Kaya walked over and sat down beside Bridget on the couch.

"I wish you'd let us meet him before you married him," their father said with a frown. "What if I don't approve of him?"

"Does it really matter?" Kaya asked. "We're married, and that's not changing anytime soon." She folded her arms over her chest, a stance that her whole family recognized as her digging her heels in. Not that any of them would favor her getting a divorce anyway.

Their mother sighed dramatically. "He was in Texas. You could have at least let us meet him."

Kaya shrugged. "He wasn't there long, and it was our honeymoon. We didn't see anyone really."

A knock at the door interrupted the conversation, and Kaya jumped up and hurried to the door. When she opened it, she smiled, throwing the door wide. "Hey, Kelsi. Are you playing welcome wagon today?"

A petite blonde walked into the cabin, a basket of fruit in her hand. "I meant to have this here before your family got here, but I had a rough morning." She waved at the Taylors. "It's so nice to meet you! I'm Kelsi Clapper, formerly Kelsi Weston. My family owns the ranch, and I run Kelsey's Kafé. I'm sure I'll see you sometime this week."

Bridget smiled. "I heard that you're a Bigfoot lover!"

Kelsi nodded. "Bigfoot lives right here in our mountains, and I aim to prove it. No matter what it takes!"

"Well, you'd better be careful now that you're pregnant. How far along *are* you?" Bridget kept a straight face when Kaya winked at her. Kaya was tall enough she was easily visible over the other woman's head.

"About six months. Do I look it?" Kelsi turned to the side and pulled her shirt closer.

"You do! I think you look beautiful!" Bridget grinned. Kaya had been right. Kelsi was thrilled to be asked about the baby. She was obviously very proud to be pregnant.

After Kelsi had left, Kaya smiled at Bridget. "You did great! Thank you!"

"I love that she believes in Bigfoot."

Kaya shook her head. "It's amazing that she still does after everything her brothers have put her through. They made a plaster cast of a huge foot, and they go up in the hills and make footprints for her to find. They have this spray that they use to make it smell like Bigfoot was around. They're really bratty to her about the whole thing, and she just takes it all in stride."

"You'd have killed me."

"No doubt!" Kaya agreed.

Another knock came to the door, and Kaya hurried off again. There was silence for a minute, and then she led a very tall man with dark hair into the room. "Mom, Dad, Bridget, this is Glen. Glen, this is my family." Kaya was holding Glen's arm as if she was afraid he'd run away if she wasn't keeping him there.

Bridget smiled. "I've heard a lot about you!"

Glen frowned. "Don't believe any of it!"

Their dad walked to him, offering his hand to shake. "It's so nice to meet you."

"You too, sir." Glen looked nervous to be meeting his in-laws, but he handled it well.

Bridget immediately wondered if there was something about their relationship that Kaya hadn't mentioned. She'd grill her later. "Thanks for having us over for supper tonight."

"I'm happy all of you were able to make it for the reception."

After Kaya and Glen had left, Bridget stood and stretched. "How long do we have before we need to leave for supper?" she asked.

"About an hour."

Bridget smiled. "I think I'll take my favorite sister's book into the hot tub and catch up on my reading. Back in a while." She loved to read Kaya's romances, but she never felt like there was enough time to do everything she wanted to do. Usually it was her pleasure reading that was thrown out the window.

After a long leisurely soak, Bridget showered and dried her hair, dressing carefully in jeans and a button up shirt. She felt like it was the right thing to wear when staying at a ranch. She usually wore her scrubs everywhere, so she didn't have a whole lot of clothes to choose from. She grabbed her coat and hurried out of her room.

When she got to the living room, her parents were waiting on her. "Ready?" her mom asked, and Bridget nodded. How she wished she was in this beautiful place alone instead of with her parents.

When they arrived at Kaya's house, Bridget immediately fell in love. It was an older ranch house, and it needed some TLC, but it just felt like it had a lot of character. "Love the place."

Kaya smiled. "We'll work on the house once Glen's business is up and running." She explained that he was starting a horse therapy ranch for autistic children, and Bridget nodded. Glen really did seem like a good guy, and she was happy for her sister. She'd never want a man that tall for herself though. He was well over a foot taller than she was! Kaya was almost a foot taller, and he was quite a bit taller than her sister.

She helped Kaya in the kitchen. "So is he coming?" Bridget asked.

"Kevin?"

Bridget nodded. "Yeah."

"Glen said he'd be here."

There was a loud knock on the door, and a minute later Glen came in with a man. "This is Kevin. He's the new pastor on the ranch."

Bridget felt her heart sink. "Pastor?" Kaya hiccupped as she tried to keep from laughing, and Bridget elbowed her in the stomach. "It's nice to meet you, Pastor." She wanted to kick her sister but managed to refrain. When she'd been in youth group as a teenager, they'd had to station someone at the exit, because she was considered a flight risk. One little "unplanned outing" to a convenience store during her youth time, and she never thought she'd live it down. Kaya knew she would never cut it as a pastor's wife. The brat!

Kevin stepped forward, taking Bridget's hand in his. "It's so nice to meet you. Kaya tells me you live in Texas."

Bridget felt a jolt of electricity at his touch. *Really? Am I so desperate I'm falling for a pastor? I know I'd make the worst pastor's wife on the entire planet.* "I do. I'm a nurse there."

"What kind of nursing do you do?"

"I work for a doctor who does family practice. I started out working in geriatrics, but I just wasn't cut out for that."

"And you like what you do now?"

Bridget shrugged. "For the most part. I like the regular

hours a lot better than I liked being up all night. That wasn't good for me." She'd always needed a very strict sleep schedule to do well, and the constantly changing hours of a nursing home had been very rough on her system.

"I hope you enjoy your time in Idaho." His eyes met hers, and she was struck by them. They were so brown! And not a mud brown either, no his reminded her of a giant chocolate kiss.

"I'm sure I will." She pulled her hand away from his grasp, flushing slightly. She wanted to get to know him better, but—*Dear God!*—he was a pastor. Nothing good could come of that. She wanted to wipe her hand off on her thigh, so his touch would not still be there, but how rude would that look?

"I'd be happy to show you around the ranch. There aren't any events except your sister's this week, so I'm pretty much on my own. I'll hold services in the little chapel in the Old West town on Sunday. Have you seen the Old West town yet?"

Bridget shook her head. "I had no idea there were services on the ranch." She went to church regularly, but she tried to sneak out quickly afterward. She tended to offend everyone with her mouth.

"Not every week, but it's offered. There are some guests who want me to preach this Sunday, so I will. It's just one of the services the ranch offers. Usually I go to church in town."

"That sounds really nice." She couldn't quit staring at his eyes. She wanted to drown in them. She wanted to throw herself in his arms and kiss him. *He's a pastor, for heaven's sake. You can't fall for him!*

"Do you like to go four-wheeling?" he asked. "I'd love to take you up into the mountains. We could do some hiking. Or if we get snow like they're predicting, maybe we could go snowmobiling."

"Would you help me search for Bigfoot?" she asked.

He nodded. "I'd love to help you search for Bigfoot. Anything you want."

She sighed. He was so nice. Too nice. He was too good for her. She caused problems; she didn't solve them. "It sounds like fun. I wouldn't mind spending some time with you before I head back to Texas." She needed him to know up front that there would be no relationship. There couldn't be. She wasn't good enough for a pastor in any way.

"I'd like nothing more. Where are you staying?"

"We're in the Bearfoot Bungalow."

"I'll walk over and pick you up in the morning. Say around nine?"

Bridget nodded slowly. She was going to get in over her head very quickly. God help her, she was falling for a pastor. She was going to kick her sister later, because she deserved it!

Chapter Two

BRIDGET WOKE EARLY the next morning, grumbling under her breath. She always woke up grumpy. More sleep was all she asked for in life, so why had she agreed to meet a man before noon on her vacation? A pastor of all people! What was Kaya thinking, trying to get her to date a pastor?

Thirty minutes later, Bridget was dressed and ready for her day. She grabbed a banana from the fruit basket, figuring that would be enough to hold her until she got back to the cabin. Her parents were off doing something—she had no idea what.

When she'd finished her breakfast, there was a knock at the door, and she hurried over to open it. As soon as she saw Kevin standing outside the door, she remembered why she was going out with him. The man made her weak in the knees.

"Hi," she said softly, staring at him.

He grinned at her. "Are you ready? You're going to need a coat. The weather's just gotten really cold in the last week."

Bridget opened the door wider. "Let me run and get a coat then. Do you think I need gloves?"

"Absolutely. It's pretty cold right now."

She didn't say it, but she was secretly excited to be able to wear winter clothes. She'd bought a new coat, gloves, and a scarf just for this trip. She bundled up and hurried out of her room, ready to take on the Idaho cold. "I'm ready."

Kevin looked up and saw Bridget all bundled up as if she was about to face the arctic and almost laughed. "I'm sure you'll be plenty warm in that getup."

"Too warm?" Bridget asked with a frown. Nothing was worse than being too warm!

"If you get too hot, you can take your coat off…or your scarf or gloves. At least we know you'll be warm enough." He opened the front door and held it for her. "I thought we could walk through the Old West town, and then we'll go over and borrow the four-wheelers."

"What's so special about the Old West town?" she asked, wishing he'd hold her hand and then mentally scolding herself for wishing it. A pastor holding your hand was like announcing you were married, wasn't it? That's not what she needed at the moment!

"You'll see." As they walked toward the town, he pointed out the RV park, the direction of the main house and the café, pool, and the golf course. "The mountains are behind us, but they're hard to miss, so I won't point them out."

"But you just did!"

"Just did what?"

"You just pointed them out?"

He sighed and shook his head. "I said I wasn't pointing them out. See the difference?"

"No!" She shook her head. "Did Kaya tell you to make me crazy?"

When they stepped into the town he'd mentioned, she felt as if she was transported back in time. "A general store! Oh, I have a mad desire to shop there!"

He grinned. "Let's!" He hurried to open the door for her, and she stepped inside, looking around. The store was heated by a small pot-bellied stove on one side, lending to the authentic feel of the place. Kevin had worked there for someone who was out sick just the week before, so he knew the place well. He wasn't exactly a lover of shopping, but if it made her happy, he'd be happy to accompany her.

A woman walked over to them, dressed in clothes that looked like she belonged in an old John Wayne movie. "May I help you?"

"Hi, Heidi." Kevin grinned at the shopkeeper. "I like the outfit. I haven't seen you wear period costume before today!"

"I haven't before today! I was thinking it would be fun and add to the atmosphere of the place. I won't wear it in summer, because it would be too hot, but it's perfect for chilly fall and winter days!"

"So it is! Have you met Bridget yet? She's Kaya's younger sister."

Bridget held her hand out for Heidi's. "Kaya and I are actually twins. She's just taller. A whole foot taller."

Heidi grinned. "I can see it in the face, but your coloring is so different. And she is a tad bit taller."

"Anyway, it's nice to meet you. I love your store!" The store seemed to be stocked with every necessity for a camping vacation. There was food, clothing, and even blankets and firewood.

"I'm kind of proud of it. If you're looking for a souvenir from your vacation, feel free to buy a post card, instead of stealing our pastor." Heidi winked at Bridget who blushed.

"I'll consider that." She wandered through the store, stopping and looking at every little thing. "Oh look! Bigfoot magnets!"

"My little sister thought those were necessary, and I argued with her, but when she digs her heels in, she's a force to be reckoned with." A tall man who must have come in right behind them, held his hand out to her. "I'm Wade Weston. I'm the manager around here."

"So nice to meet you." Bridget had an insane urge to curtsey, but she managed to restrain herself. "Love the store, and our cabin is fabulous. I'm Kaya's little sister."

Wade nodded. "Kaya's nice. She and Glen seem very happy."

"I'm here for the reception."

"I hope you enjoy your time at River's End." Wade walked over to talk to Heidi. "I love the costume. We made need to make the others wear them!"

"If you do, don't blame it on me. Please!"

Bridget shook her head with a grin. She understood what Heidi was worried about exactly. At her old nursing home, one of the nurses had showed up at work in one of the old-fashioned white nursing uniforms like they'd worn in the seventies and eighties. The director of nursing had liked it and suggested everyone wear them, and the rest of the nurses had gotten annoyed. No one wanted to mess with that nonsense when scrubs were available.

Bridget picked up a couple of small magnets to purchase. She loved having a refrigerator that looked like she'd been all over the world, when really, she'd rarely been out of Texas. She paid for her items, and she and Kevin left the store.

"For a friend back home?" he asked, nodding at

her bag.

"One for me and one for my friend, Jenni. I don't think she's ever been to Idaho." Jenni's family was more likely to go to Europe on a vacation than a Western state.

Next door to the mercantile was an apothecary shop, and Bridget stopped short. "An old-fashioned apothecary? My nurse's heart is beating faster just looking at it! Are we allowed to go in?"

Kevin laughed and opened the door. "This is the first-aid station on the ranch. There's a full-time nurse who works here."

An older woman with gray hair and dark blue eyes descended the stairs, stopping at the bottom. "Are you just looking or does someone need me?"

"We're just looking," Kevin called back.

"Actually, I'd like to pick your brain for a minute if you don't mind," Bridget said, a smile on her face. "I've heard you're retiring, and I'm an RN. This place is amazing, and my sister just married Glen…"

"So you're thinking about applying for my job, and want to know what's entailed?" The nurse came to the bottom of the staircase and waved a hand toward a very modern-looking first aid area. "Have a seat, and we'll talk."

Bridget hurried over to sit in the visitor's chair, and sensed that Kevin walked up behind her. After Emily was seated, Bridget asked, "Tell me what your job entails."

"You name it, it's there. I treat people for altitude sickness more than anything. Lots of people for dehydration, because they don't pack enough water and go walking the mountains. Minor injuries. I decide if someone needs to be sent off to the nearest hospital, or if I can treat them here. I've dealt with panic attacks. At the moment my most frequent patient is Kelsi. She's convinced her baby is going to be an alien-Bigfoot crossbreed and has lots of questions."

Bridget grinned. "I can picture her thinking that."

"Girl's a mess, but I love her. I've been here since before she was born." Emily put her hand to her back. "I lived in town until my husband died, and then we renovated the upstairs of this place into a small apartment for me. It works, but it's nothing fancy."

Bridget bit her lip. She loved the idea of working at this beautiful ranch, and the opportunity to live above an old-time apothecary shop would make her so happy! "How many hours do you work?"

Emily shrugged. "It really varies. We're open year-round, so there's always something going on. I'm more 'on call' than anything else. I sometimes teach first aid classes to new employees. Everyone here has to be CPR-certified, and I'm licensed to teach it. I vary from twenty-five to forty hours per week, I think. I haven't tracked it in years. I'm just here when I'm needed."

"And who would I talk to about applying for your position? How soon are you thinking of retiring?"

"I'm ready to retire. I'd retire tomorrow if there was someone to take my place."

Bridget bit her lip. "I can't give my notice until I get back to Texas, and that's if I decide to apply. I'll think on it."

After they'd left the building, Kevin looked down at her with new interest. If she was thinking of staying, maybe they could have a real relationship. He'd love that!

As soon as they stepped outside, Bridget caught the scent of fresh-baked bread. "Oh, something smells yummy!"

Kevin just laughed and shook his head. She certainly had no problem being herself in front of a man she barely knew. He followed as she spotted the bakery and hurried to it, opening the door and leaving him standing in the street.

Inside, Bridget wandered to the display case, her nose twitching with happiness. "I want one of everything!"

The girl behind the counter smiled. "I can box that up for you, but are you sure you can eat that much?"

Kevin walked up behind her, shaking his head. "Maybe you could choose two things and we'll have them for dessert later."

"But what will *you* eat?" Bridget winked at him as she contemplated for a moment before nodding. "I guess that's enough. Could I pick two different things and we split them, though?"

He grinned. "Sure. Any two things would thrill me."

Bridget looked through everything in the case three times. "Choosing is hard! I'll be here every day until I go home! I promise you!"

"I'm Miranda. I have a feeling we're going to be friends if you're here every day!" The girl behind the counter grinned. "How long are you here for?"

"Just a week. I'm getting the impression it won't be long enough. My sister married Glen, though, so I'll be back."

"I like Kaya." Miranda smiled. "We'll happily feed you every day. We're not open Sundays, though."

"I'll just buy double on Saturday then. Thank you for helping me plan my week." Finally, Bridget pointed. "I want a cream cheese brownie and that cupcake with the purple icing. That looks amazing!"

"That's a white cupcake with huckleberry butter cream frosting."

"Oh, yeah. I could eat my weight in that." Bridget happily waited while Miranda put them in a bag. "Thank you so much!"

Kevin stepped forward to pay, and Bridget frowned. He hadn't gotten a choice, so he shouldn't have to pay. "I can pay for it!"

"We're sharing, so I get to pay." He handed Miranda some cash and waited for his change. "Thanks, Miranda."

"You're welcome. I'll see you again…"

"Bridget!" Bridget turned and smiled. "By the end of the week we'll be life-long friends, so knowing each other's names is probably important."

Miranda laughed and waved. "See you tomorrow!"

Just before she reached the door, Bridget spun around again. "Miranda, I need to know…something. It's *very* important!"

Miranda frowned. "Okay, what is it?"

"Cinderella or Belle?" Bridget could feel Kevin's stare. He must think she'd lost her mind. No matter. She wasn't sure she could be lifelong friends with someone who chose Belle over Cinderella, so it was vitally important.

"Cinderella. Who else could it be? I mean, it's the classic fairy tale!"

"Yup, we're going to be great friends!" Bridget stepped outside looking around her. "Where's the saloon? What's an Old West town without a saloon?"

"It's down across the street from the mercantile. You were so busy being excited about the apothecary that you missed it."

Bridget frowned. "Well, what's inside?" She'd already figured out that the shops weren't always what they seemed on the outside.

"It's really an old-fashioned looking saloon type place, but they have a soda shop. Fancy coffee, sodas, and ice cream. Want to try it?"

She bit her lip for a moment before nodding. "Would

you mind? I don't really need to eat there, but I want to see it!"

"Then let's go." Kevin loved to watch her excitement at the place. He'd been just as in love with it when he'd first come to the ranch. History had always appealed to him, and he couldn't help but be sucked into the magic of the town there. He pointed out a huge tree, off behind the row of houses behind her. "That tree was the tree the original Westons decorated at Christmastime when they moved here. And that house belonged to Frankie Weston…the matriarch of the Weston family."

"Wait…the matriarch was named Frankie?"

"Yup. Her real name was Francine, but she pretended to be a boy until she sent for a mail order groom. She was a bit ahead of her time."

"Sounds like it! Do you know when that was?"

Kevin shrugged. "I've heard a couple of different things. Some say it was in the 1880s…some say the 1890s. I'm not sure what the real story is, but I'm doing some research on my time off to put it together. I'm going to gather as much as I can, and have Kaya write out a history of the ranch for me."

"She can do it. My sister is the best writer around. I'm surprised she'd agree to write something non-fiction though. She hates non-fiction."

"She did ask if she could fictionalize it and write it as a romance. I probably should have told her no, but I was so excited that she was going to do it, I said yes."

"So my sister is going to write a romance novel about the history of this ranch. That sounds like Kaya. What's she going to call it?"

He frowned, wracking his brain. "I think she said *Mail Order Miracle*? Something like that. I'm not sure."

"I'm sure she'll tell me when it's out."

"Do you read her work?"

Bridget nodded. "Not always, but I try to when I have time to spare."

"Am I going to blush if I try to read it?"

"Probably not. She doesn't get too terribly naughty with her books." Next to the saloon was a sign propped up against the side of the building. She tilted her head so she could read it. "Sadie's Soda Saloon." She watched as he opened the saloon door. As soon as she was inside, she grinned. There was a long wooden bar to the left with barstools and a flight of stairs to the right. "I love this place!"

"Me too!" he said with a grin. "I like to hang out here and write my sermons sometimes."

She frowned at the thought of him being a pastor. "Did you always want to be a pastor?"

He shook his head. "Nope. My upbringing wasn't super religious, but when I finished college, I realized what I wanted more than anything was to help people. I had become involved in a local mission during college, and I decided to go to seminary. I'm actually more versed in counseling than I am in preaching, but I can do either. The ranch hired me on to perform weddings, but I preach once every three or four weeks."

"I see. But you don't really have a congregation, right?"

"Not really. I actually do a lot to help with different things around the ranch. If someone calls in sick or a department is short-handed for a bit, I'll come in and work. I love the diversity of not having to do the same thing every day. I have to show you my little church."

Bridget noticed there were a few people there, sipping coffee. "I'm not thirsty or anything, but this place is cool."

"Go ahead and look around. Sadie won't mind."

"Sadie?"

He gestured to the woman behind the bar. “Am I allowed to go upstairs?”

Sadie shook her head. “No, it’s just storage up there. Stay down here.”

Bridget spun in a slow circle looking at everything around her. “I want to live here when I grow up.”

Kevin laughed. “I’m happy to help you make that happen.”

They stopped at the church next, and it was just what Bridget thought an old-time church should be. It had stained glass windows, hard wooden pews, and a pulpit at the front. She sank into one of the pews. “Preach it!”

He was startled for a moment, but how could he resist? He walked to the front and talked softly about the love of God. After five minutes, he was done, and he came out and sat beside her. “Are you a Christian, Bridget?”

She nodded. “I am. Not a very good one, I’m afraid, but I am.”

“Why aren’t you a good one?” he asked, frowning.

“Good Christians don’t offend people. I have a hard time opening my mouth without being offensive.”

“I haven’t noticed that. And a lot of good Christians offend people.”

She shrugged, not wanting to get more into it. “I love your town, and this little church. This really must be an amazing place to work. Especially for a history buff.”

He frowned, not wanting to change the subject, but he nodded. “I wouldn’t trade my life here for anything.”

She thought for a moment he might kiss her, but he just looked into her eyes. His hair was dark and his eyes were a deep brown, and Bridget just wanted to melt into them. He was so incredibly sexy…it was wasted on a pastor in Bridget’s opinion.

“Let’s walk,” he said. “Are you hungry? I thought I’d

get us boxed lunches to eat on the trail, but it's already past one. We took a long time in the town."

"Yeah, I'm very hungry. Isn't there supposed to be a café here or something?" She put her hand over her eyes and looked around. There had been a diner in the "town" but he said it wasn't open at the moment.

"Yes, Kelsey's Kafé. It was named after the grandmother of the Kelsi who currently runs it. The grandmother opened it, and taught Kelsi everything she knows." He walked beside her, stealing glances out of the corner of his eye. Why was he so attracted to this crazy little woman? He was certain he'd seen her stab her sister with a tiny fork the previous evening, but both sisters had just laughed, so could that have been what happened?

"I met Kelsi last night. She's really fun!"

"She is! Is she the reason you want to hunt for Bigfoot?"

"She inspired it, but I love the idea. I mean, who wouldn't want to hunt for Bigfoot?"

Kevin shrugged at that, stopping in front of a building with a huge sign reading, "Kelsey's Kafé."

"What's good here?" she asked as they went in and found a booth off to one side.

Kelsi herself came to the table immediately. "Everything's good! Bob is the best cook in all of Idaho. Maybe in all of the world, but don't tell him I said that or he might get a big head, and what would we do with a big-headed cook?"

Bridget grinned. "Lop off his ears and serve them as an appetizer?"

"I like the way you think! Just enough gruesome details to make me smile. Do you like horror films?"

Bridget nodded emphatically. "I love them! You?"

"Oh, yeah! You two should come over for a movie

night. How's tomorrow night?"

Bridget shrugged. "I think the only day I'm booked is Saturday. Today's what? Tuesday? I always lose track of my days on vacation."

"Yeah, it's Tuesday. Well?"

"Sure. I'm game!"

Kelsi looked at Kevin who squirmed a bit. "I've never really been into horror films."

Kelsi rolled her eyes. "Then you and Shane can sit around talking about guy stuff while we girls watch them. Don't be a pain, Pastor Kevin."

Kevin shrugged. "I can hang out with Shane, I guess."

"Good. I'll make my famous enchiladas. Do you like hot or burn your tongue off and never recover scorching?"

Bridget shrugged. "I would probably prefer hot, but Kaya would be all about burning her tongue off."

"Yeah, we like the same brand of Cajun seasoning! We discovered that when she first got here."

"Of course you do." Bridget shook her head. "She said you two got along very well. I should have guessed."

"Does this mean that you won't eat our Cajun seasoning topped everything with us?" Kelsi asked, her eyes wide.

"Nope. Maybe I should meet *your* twin, since you love mine so much."

Kelsi smiled. "I'm sure you will! It's a big ranch, but the whole family will be at Glen and Kaya's reception. I'll make sure I introduce you."

"Kaya said you guys are identical."

Kelsi shrugged. "We were at one point. Her hair is shorter and darker. And she's much thinner. No protrusions." Kelsi patted her pleasantly rounded belly. The clothes she was wearing showed her belly off more than the clothes from the previous day.

Bridget laughed. "So tell me what to order."

"Special today is a taco burger, served with a small mountain of fried cheese curds."

Bridget handed the menu back to Kelsi without blinking. "You sold me."

Kevin looked back and forth between the two women. He was pleased Bridget got along with everyone so quickly. "I'll take the special as well. No need to hurt Bob's feelings."

Kelsi rolled her eyes. "Like Bob has feelings." She raised her voice as she said it.

From the kitchen, Bridget heard a gruff voice say, "One of us has to be able to keep a stiff upper lip while the other one cries and blames it on pregnancy hormones!"

Bridget giggled softly. The place was pretty full, but no one blinked an eye. They must all be regulars.

"I'll go put this in. Back in a few."

Kelsi hurried off, and Bridget turned her attention to Kevin. It was the first time he'd sat across from her, and she was suddenly at a loss for words. *Why does he have to be a pastor? Why? Why? Why?*

"Are you and Kaya close?" Kevin asked, nodding at Kelsi to thank her for putting the water in front of him. He had to say something to break the silence. Bridget suddenly seemed incapable of speech.

Bridget shrugged. "I don't think we're as close as most twins. I mean, we love each other. I can't think of anyone I love more than my sister, but we don't always get along great. We don't exactly share a brain or anything."

"Why don't you get along?"

Bridget shrugged. "She gets on my nerves. I get on her nerves. We have no siblings other than each other, and I think sometimes we just are around each other too much and annoy each other." She sighed. "And we disagree on the most fundamental of all things—who the best Disney princess is. I say it's good old Cindy, but she says Belle. How could a book worm be the best Disney princess, I ask you?"

"Cindy?"

"Cinderella of course. Please tell me you received a proper education and you've seen all the Disney movies."

"I—well—I've seen more Disney movies than I have horror films. That should count for something, shouldn't it?"

She frowned at him. "We'll get you educated before I leave. I'm sure there's a library of movies to borrow from here. I read about it on the website." She sighed. "You'll choose before I go, won't you?"

He laughed. "If I absolutely need to, I will."

"What about you? Any siblings?"

He shook his head. "Nope. Don't even know my parents. I was raised on a Boys' Ranch in Nowhere, Texas. It was a nice place, but it was for kids who the system had failed or who were in so much trouble their parents didn't know what to do with them. My parents dumped me there as a baby, and they took me in."

"I'm sorry." Her hand covered his on the middle of the table, and she immediately wanted to remove it when she realized who she was with. Had they just declared their engagement?

"Nothing to be sorry about. It was a great place to grow up. I was loved, and I doubt I would have been with my parents. Otherwise, they wouldn't have given me up."

"I guess not." It was odd…thinking of him as a young boy alone tugged on her heart strings more than she would have expected. And when he turned his hand over and gripped hers, her stomach flipped and flopped. She was in trouble. Bad trouble. Why did he have to be a pastor?

Chapter Three

WHEN KELSI CAME BACK to the table a few minutes later, Bridget asked her the question she asked any woman she was contemplating having for a friend. The most important question she knew. "Cinderella or Belle?"

Kelsi grinned as she placed their water on the table. "That's easy. Belle, of course. Who would like someone else?"

Bridget made a face. "I do. I think Cinderella is the perfect Disney heroine for any era. She's the one whose story is retold again and again. Any writer who knows how to use a keyboard rewrites Cindy's story. Not that many rewrite Belle's."

Kelsi frowned, her hands on her hips. "Don't make me throw you out of my place, Bridget. You know as well as I do that Cinderella is just a Belle-wannabe. Don't try and make me mad. I'm pregnant and hormonal!"

Kevin looked back and forth between Kelsi and Bridget. Bridget's face was turning a little red, but she sat back and crossed her arms across her chest. "Fine. Be on the wrong side."

Kelsi sighed. "How does Kaya feel?"

Bridget wrinkled her nose. "She's on the wrong side too."

"Might is right." With that, Kelsi turned on her heel and walked back to the counter where she was refilling the salt shakers from all the tables. She kept looking up at Bridget and mumbling something under her breath, but she said nothing else Bridget and Kevin could actually hear.

Kevin looked at Bridget as if she'd lost her mind, because he wasn't sure that she hadn't. "Why are you picking fights with people about who the best Disney Princess is?"

Bridget shrugged. "It's just my thing. I have a favorite princess, and I think everyone else should love the same one."

"That's a bit crazy, you know."

"I never claimed to be sane." She dug a tiny fork out of the pocket of her jeans. "Would a sane woman carry a shrimp fork everywhere for the express purpose of stabbing her sister?"

"I thought I saw you with a shrimp fork! Why do you have that?"

"I told you. I carry it so I can stab Kaya with it. It keeps us from arguing so much."

He frowned for a moment, not wanting to ask, but… "How does that keep you from arguing with her?"

"If she starts to get on my nerves, I stab her. If I get on her nerves she stabs me. There's a whole lot of stabbing going on, but no one is *really* getting hurt, and we're not wanting to kill each other because of disagreements either. See? It makes sense."

"So basically, you take out your aggression on your sister by stabbing her?"

Bridget nodded emphatically. "We were on a cruise together recently, and we were annoying our friend, Jenni. We discovered the shrimp fork trick by accident, but it was fabulous. Of course, we ate all our meals with our tiny shrimp forks and annoyed the waiters, but we tipped extra to make up for it."

Kevin stared at her. He was very attracted, but he worried she may need a mental health professional. "How exactly does Kaya feel about this?"

"We got each other boxes of shrimp forks. We seriously got each other the same gifts." She frowned down at hers. "Of course, I got hers with Cinderella on the end, and she got mine with Belle, which is really a dirty rotten trick."

"Have you sought out professional help?"

Bridget laughed, the sound filling up the diner. "I thought about it, but I'm as sane as the next person. I just found a way to take out my aggression on my sister without it eating away at me."

"I guess." He shook his head. "I've never heard of anyone doing anything like that before."

"I shipped nerf guns ahead. If she makes me really mad, I'll give her a gun and three hundred ammunition, and I'll take the same. We'll warn everyone there's a war going on and just make it happen."

He shook his head. How did a sane person respond? He did remember summers when tensions ran high on the boys' ranch when they would each be given a squirt gun with a jug of water filled with food coloring. Each boy would get a new white shirt, and they'd run around shooting each other and creating shirts with one of a kind designs. It was a way to get out their aggressions without hurting anyone. Why couldn't adults do it too? Think of the lives that could be saved if the rulers of opposing countries were given shrimp forks instead of armies. Maybe she was onto something.

"Do you want to go up in the mountains on four-wheelers after lunch?"

"What time is it?" she asked.

He pulled out his phone and checked. "Just after two."

Kelsi put their plates in front of them. "No need to hurry, but we're going to be closing up shop around you."

Bridget frowned. "I had no idea you were closing! Do you want us to take them to go?"

"Of course not!" Kelsi shook her head. "You two eat. It'll be a while before we're done with everything anyway."

Bridget grabbed one of the cheese curds and popped it into her mouth, immediately fanning it with her hand. "Hot!" She took a huge gulp of her water. "But good!"

He frowned at the cheese curd. "I've honestly never had these. What exactly is a cheese curd anyway?"

"Mom is from Wisconsin, so I grew up eating them. She says they're what's left in the vat after the cheese is made. Doesn't sound terribly appetizing when you phrase it that way, but it's so good!" She popped another into her mouth and immediately fanned it with her hand again. "You distracted me and made me forget how hot they were!"

He picked one up, turned it over in his hand, and then dipped it in ranch. "I bet it would cool off if you dipped it." He put the whole thing into his mouth as she had, chewing slowly. "These are really good!"

She nodded. "Better without adulteration. Why would you put ranch on something that's already delicious?"

"Because it's here, and I like to dip!"

"Well, break the habit, man! Try the real thing. I promise it's delicious!"

He shook his head at her bossiness, but picked up

another cheese curd and bit into it without the ranch. It burned his tongue a bit, but she was right. "It *is* better."

"Told you." She picked up her taco burger and bit into it, a small piece of taco meat sliding out. "That's pretty good too."

He eyed his burger. He usually just got a sandwich, but he'd wanted to be adventurous after hearing her order. "You sure? It won't poison me?"

"If you didn't want to try it, why did you order it?"

He shrugged, feeling a bit stupid. "Seemed like a good idea at the time."

"You ordered it, now you have to eat it." She gave him a look, making it clear he wasn't going to get out of trying at least one bite.

He picked up the burger and bit into it warily. "Hey, this isn't too bad."

She rolled her eyes. "I don't understand, but I'm not going to say anything else."

He took a sip of his water. "You never answered my question earlier. Are you still up for a trip into the mountains?"

"Do we have time? It's already after two…"

He sighed. "Probably not. Sun sets around 4:30."

"Then we'll do it another time."

"Tomorrow?"

She grinned. "Sure. Why not? We should find a place to watch movies too. I think someone needs a little Cindy and Belle in his life."

"You're going to make me watch kids' movies?"

"They're not kids' movies! They're Disney princess movies. That's like saying that Star Trek is a sci-fi show, when it changed a whole generation of television viewers!"

He didn't want her to get started on Star Trek. He was a huge fan, but she didn't need to know that. Not yet anyway. Her obsession with Disney princesses was kind of scary. He was waiting for her to spout that nonsense about Princess Leia from Star Wars being a Disney princess now, and he would go toe to toe with her on that one. He didn't much care about which princess was best out of Cinderella or Belle, though. "I guess we can do that. There's a library in the main house for guests with a whole selection of movies. I think most are family friendly."

"When will we do that then?"

He shrugged. "When do you want to do it? We could also watch a movie on the television in your guest cabin, but the only one that has the streaming functionality is the one in the living room, and I'm not sure how I feel about dating with your parents watching." He'd spent a week in the cabin when he'd first gotten to the ranch, so it was very familiar to him.

Bridget cocked her head to one side, studying Kevin. "Are we dating then?"

"I don't know what else to call it. A stupendously tame wild vacation fling?"

"Why stupendously tame?"

"Because just wild would imply all kinds of sexual shenanigans, and as a pastor, I don't do that before marriage. So it'll have to be stupendously tame instead of wild."

She sighed. "I guess we can do the stupendously tame thing then. I might demand a kiss or two."

"Kisses will be expected." Kevin winked at her as he ate another bite of his burger.

Once they were finished, he quickly paid and they left the restaurant, walking in the direction of her cabin. "Do you want to watch something in the main house?"

She shrugged. "Sounds good. We could do Disney

tonight and horror flicks tomorrow night. Both ends of the spectrum."

"You're on." He frowned, thinking about the best way to do it. "Do you need to check in with your parents?"

She sighed. "I should. I've been on my own for five years, but I still need to check in with Mom and Dad before I go on a date on my vacation. It just made sense for me to share a place with them and not pay for my own!"

"I'll come back around seven then. I'll bring a pizza and some popcorn. We'll watch movies, and you can tell me why you're so sure that Cindy is better than Belle."

She put her hand on the doorknob, but he stopped her, leaning down to gently kiss her cheek.

"I'll be back in a few hours." Kevin turned and walked away, and she stared after him. His bottom looked good in his tight jeans. Was it okay for a girl to notice a pastor's butt? She didn't know, and at the moment she just didn't care. If it was wrong, then she didn't care about doing the right thing. How could she with a butt like that?

She went in and sat down on the couch, where her parents were talking. "What did you guys do today?" They'd been gone before she woke up, and she realized she had no idea at all where they'd been.

Her dad smiled. "We rented a boat and went out on the lake. Caught some trout, but I threw them back. Your mother said she wasn't spending her whole evening cleaning and cooking fish when there was a perfectly good restaurant here on the ranch."

Bridget wasn't surprised. Her mother had never been overly fond of cooking. "Sounds good to me. So you guys are going to the restaurant?"

Her mother frowned. "I thought we'd all go together."

"Kevin and I are going to watch *Cinderella* and *Beauty and the Beast*. He needs to choose."

"You're not dragging him into that silly argument you used to have with your sister, are you? Nobody cares who the better princess is!"

"I do. Kaya does. Jenni does. Kelsi does. Miranda does."

Her mother frowned at her. "Who on earth is Miranda?" She'd met Jenni and Kelsi, but Miranda was a new name.

"She runs the bakery in the Old West town. Her baked goods look wonderful. I'm going to get two desserts from there every day." Bridget frowned, realizing Kevin had absconded with their desserts. He'd better remember to bring them to the movie!

"You and your sweet tooth. All right. You have fun watching your movie."

"I'm going to get my nap." Bridget stood and yawned widely. Her one complaint about being a nurse was there were no nap times. She'd seriously considered moving somewhere they had mandatory naps in the middle of the day. Naps weren't just for babies! They were for everyone, and should be embraced by the general populace.

"Sleep well," her father said.

As Bridget walked away, she could hear her parents whispering, but she didn't care. They could talk about her all day. She was going to have a wonderful evening with a good man. What else mattered?

She quickly changed into her pajamas and crawled between the sheets, yawning widely. She was excited about seeing Kevin again, but even more excited about napping first. She would never understand children. Didn't they understand that naps were a gift from God?

The last thing on her mind as she drifted off was the confusion on Kevin's face when she'd brought up the princesses to first Miranda and then Kelsi. Eventually he'd understand the way her mind worked, and when he did, he'd either propose on the spot or run screaming into the night. There could be no in between.

She smiled. *Yessirree, Kevin was in for the ride of his life.*

* * *

Kevin let himself into his small apartment in Riston, locking the door behind him. He wasn't sure why he was locking doors, except that he'd gotten into the habit when he'd gone to seminary. His school hadn't been in the safest area of town.

He sank into a chair and stared bemusedly at the wall. Bridget was something else. He wasn't sure if he should get far, far away, or just embrace her silliness. Either way, he was very intrigued, and all he could think about was getting to know her better.

He'd never met anyone quite like her, and he was certain he wouldn't again. The woman was nothing if not original. He would continue to pursue a relationship with her, because he couldn't seem to help himself. Not since he was in high school and had hormones coming out his nose and ears had he felt so much for one small woman. Surely if he felt that much, they were meant to be together. If not, how could God have put her in his path?

He sighed contentedly. He'd found the woman God meant for him to marry. Now he just had to convince her she was that woman. It couldn't be too hard, could it? She seemed like the perfect bride for a too-serious pastor.

Chapter Four

BRIDGET WAS WAITING when Kevin arrived. Her parents were already gone, having decided to go to the restaurant and eat and do some dancing. When she'd been a teenager, her parents had always embarrassed her with their constant dancing. In the living room, at wedding receptions, anywhere there was a dancefloor, they were dancing together, and it wasn't just slow dances. Oh, they did their share of dancing cheek to cheek, but more often than not, Dad was spinning Mom around like she was a top. It was crazy. Cute, but crazy. They were in their forties. What if one of them broke a hip?

She locked the cabin and followed him out to his car, a rusty old pile of bolts. She didn't care. She'd never judged a man by his car.

He drove them the short distance across the ranch to the main house in silence. When they'd arrived, she looked at him in surprise. She'd thought this was the main house, but it was close enough she'd figured she was wrong. Why had they driven?

"Why didn't we walk?"

He shrugged. "It's a lot colder at night, and I didn't want you to get too chilly. You're not used to the cold night air yet."

"And you are? You said you were raised in Texas." Surely he was no more used to the cold of Idaho than she was. Their Texas blood was too thin for the extreme colds of the north.

"I was, but I went to seminary in Wyoming. I've been in the north for long enough to be used to the weather here."

He reached into the back seat and pulled out a pizza bag—the kind a pizza delivery person carries. "Where'd you get *that*?"

"On eBay, of course. There's nowhere else that you could buy one. We had lots of pizza nights at seminary, and someone always had to go and pick up the pizzas, because it saved us a couple of bucks, and we were all perpetually broke. I got sick of cold pizzas, and I found this for five bucks on eBay. That was all she wrote."

Bridget shook her head, laughing. "I shouldn't be surprised, but somehow, I am."

"You were never a broke college student?"

"I definitely was, but I never thought of buying a pizza bag off eBay. I went to school in a big city, though, and we usually walked to the nearest pizza place. Or had pizza on campus."

He grabbed her hand and pulled her toward the front door of the house. "I hope no one's using the library, because I can't get my Disney princess on if I have to watch *Die Hard* or something manly like that."

"*Die Hard*? Really?"

He shrugged. "That's what my friends liked. I never really was a fan, but I've got it memorized anyway."

"You need some Disney princesses, then. Very badly."

He pushed open the door of the library, and she found a light switch. The room was dark. "Are you sure we're allowed to just come in here?"

He nodded. "I talked to Wade about it when I first got here, and he said this was for anyone to use." He could have taken her back to his place, but he didn't think it was right for a pastor to have a woman in his house if no one else was there. He tried to live by a strict moral code, so no one could come to any erroneous conclusions. Besides, he still felt awfully hormonal around her, and he didn't want anything to inadvertently happen.

He put the pizza down, along with the bag in his other hand filled with plates, napkins, forks, and the baked goods she'd bought earlier, while she went to work looking through all the titles in the library. The walls were filled with shelves. The shelves seemed to be equally divided between movies and books. It took her just a moment to locate both movies, because they were alphabetical.

She popped the first in, and sat down, picking up the remote. "I'm saving the best for last, so we'll start with *Beauty and the Beast*. It's a good movie, but it's not *Cinderella*."

He sat down beside her, taking the pizza box out of the carrier and serving them each a piece. "You didn't say what you like on pizza, so I went with a basic cheeseburger pizza. I would think anyone would love that." He pulled a couple of bottles of water from the bag, and handed her one, twisting the top off his and taking a swig.

The opening credits came on the screen, and Bridget's whole face lit up. It was as if she was seeing the movie for the first time. He wanted to laugh at her, but how could he? She was adorable in her love for Disney.

By the time *Beauty and the Beast* was done, she was nestled up close to him, and his arm was around her shoulders. He liked it. Maybe too much, but he sure wasn't going to complain. As the closing credits played on the television, she swiped at the tears in her eyes. "See? It's a good movie, but there's something so perfect about *Cinderella*. Belle makes me a little bit crazy. She's kind of a know-it-all."

He hadn't gotten that from the movie, but that was fine with him. If she wanted to think of Belle as a know-it-all, more power to her. "I liked it. I think I've seen it before, because some of the songs were familiar, but I'm really not sure."

Bridget shook her head at him. "Your education is so lacking. My heart aches for you." She jumped up, swapping out the DVDs. "Now, for the best movie of the evening." She sat down and snuggled close to him again. His arm came around her shoulders, and she settled her head against him. Never had a man made her feel so… protected as Kevin did.

She sighed. It could never last. He was a pastor who lived in Idaho, and she was a nurse from Texas. How could anyone think it might last?

Kevin stroked his hand up and down her arm. Her delicate bone structure brought out his protectiveness. She was special, and he was going to keep her. How could he not?

"You'll see right away that Cinderella is better. She communes with the animals and not just the household items!"

He forced his attention back to the television with real effort. He wanted to stare at her, not Cinderella.

As she had with the first movie, she sang along with all the songs—loudly and off-key. She seemed to genuinely enjoy singing, and he didn't mind. He was mostly tone-deaf anyway. Her voice wasn't bad, but she couldn't seem to hit a note for anything. In between songs, they shared the two desserts she'd chosen at the bakery, each of them using one of her tiny shrimp forks.

When the movie was over, she shut the television off with the remote in her hand, turning to him and tucking her legs under her on the couch. "I'm glad you didn't complain about my singing. I know I'm not good, but I make up for my lack of skills with sheer volume."

"You do!" He grinned at her, his hand stroking her cheek.

"Well? Have you made up your mind yet?"

He frowned. "Do I have to decide tonight? Both women have a lot going for them. Cindy was great with the animals, just like you said, but did you see Belle stick up for the Beast? The whole town was ready to kill him, and she not only didn't buckle under peer pressure, but she did everything she could to save him." He shook his head. "I'm just not sure I can make that kind of decision on such short notice."

Bridget rolled her eyes. "You know Cindy is better!"

"I know no such thing. I'm going to have to think on it. Analyze both storylines, and think about the songs that were sung by each of them. Belle's songs were a bit better." Not that he'd heard them over her caterwauling, but it was better to hold out and make her wait for his answer. He was sure she'd continue to see him until she got it.

She glared at him for a moment. "You're really going to make me wait to hear which your favorite is? Are you kidding me?"

He shook his head. "I'm sure I'll have made a decision before it's time for you to go home to Texas."

She frowned, her eyes meeting his. "I already hate the idea of going home. This place—it grows on you. I want to stay here forever."

"Apply for the nursing job. I sure wouldn't complain!"

She sighed. "I have to think about it. I've never lived outside of Texas. I'd be leaving my home and everything I know. My parents. My best friend."

"You would. But your sister is here. The ranch is here, and you can't deny how wonderful this ranch is. And…not to elevate myself in your eyes, but *I'm* here. I want you to stay, Bridget."

She frowned. "I'll think about it while you think about which princess you like better. You know it really does matter to me which one you choose. What if we're not compatible?"

"I don't think Disney movies are the most important things in compatibility."

"Oh, you don't? What is the most important thing?"

He shrugged. "I don't know. Feelings about faith and God. Kissing."

She let out a short bark of laughter. "Kissing, huh?"

He nodded emphatically. "How will we know if we're meant to be together if we don't have chemistry? No, I think kissing will tell us a whole lot about whether or not we are compatible."

"Oh, yeah?"

He nodded. "So, how about it? Wanna see if we're compatible?"

She tilted her head to one side with her lips pursed. "I don't know. When you kiss a pastor, are you then required to marry him so you won't sully his name and make him look like he's easy?"

He laughed. "Nope. But if you touch any bare skin that should be under clothes it does. So you can't even touch my bare back, because that belongs under my clothes, you see." He was amazed at how easily he could banter with this woman. Always he'd been tongue-tied around girls, and way too serious. Suddenly he felt like that was gone, and he could have fun.

"I'll be sure to keep my hands on the outside of your shirt then."

"And no touching below the waist even on top of my clothes! I think we'd both be struck by lightning for that one. And then we'd have to get married, because that's how pastor's wives get pregnant, you see."

Bridget nodded as if he was imparting great wisdom to her. "I'm so glad you taught me this. I was sure pastor's wives got pregnant the same way regular women did. Now I'll know what I should and shouldn't do if I want to have a baby."

"Does that mean you're marrying me?"

She laughed softly. "You can't trick me like that."

"Just get over here and kiss me, Bridget the Midget."

"Hey! You can't call me that!"

"Your sister does." He didn't wait any longer, and instead he leaned forward and gently brushed his lips across hers. The tingling that accompanied the kiss gave him a bit of a shock. He wanted…more. So much *more*. He really did want this sweetly insane woman for his bride.

Bridget blinked up at him a couple of times, her world having changed in the thirty seconds that their lips had touched. She wanted nothing more than to really touch him inside his clothes. She wanted so much. *Wow. He's a pastor. Why don't I care?*

He cleared his throat, unable to pull his gaze from hers. "I think I should get you back to your parents. I have a lot to think about."

She nodded. "I think we both do."

He hoped she meant that she was thinking about taking the nursing job at the ranch, because he wanted to spend his life with her. He knew you weren't supposed to be able to tell that when you'd only known someone for a little over twenty-four hours...wow…had he really just met her yesterday? But he did. She was his. Forever wouldn't be long enough.

Together they cleaned up the mess they'd made and put the movies back in their proper alphabetized spots. Bridget shrugged into her coat, avoiding eye contact with him. Her life was different now, but she couldn't just tell him that, could she? She would have with any other man, but no other man would have believed her. That's where Kevin was different.

He opened the door and shut the light off, walking toward his car with her at his side. Where she should always be.

They drove back to the Bearfoot Bungalow in silence, and when he walked her to the door, he briefly touched his lips to her cheek. He couldn't kiss her lips again tonight. It would be too much.

Bridget leaned back against the door, feeling like she was in a daze. She needed chocolate. And ice cream. Chocolate ice cream. How else would she be able to think?

Walking to the kitchen, she opened the freezer and found a gallon of her favorite chocolate marshmallow. She didn't bother with a bowl, but ate it right out of the container. She was in love. And he was a pastor she'd only known for a day. Had she lost her ever-loving mind?

* * *

Bridget was ready at ten the next morning. Her parents were already gone for the day, her mother choosing to spend it with Kaya, while Dad was spending the day with Glen in the stable there on the ranch.

When the knock came, she hurried to open the door,

but she couldn't meet his eyes. She could barely speak to him.

"I thought we'd start with the four-wheelers this time. We'll grab them and drive over to the café so that Kelsi can fix us up with lunches. How does that sound?"

Bridget frowned. "Did you forget about seeing my lifelong friend Miranda for dessert?"

Kevin groaned, running his hand over the back of his neck. "I guess I was kind of wishing you'd forget."

"Are you trying to deprive me of delicious sweet treats from the bakery? You *fiend!*"

"No, of course not. We just don't have a ton of time today."

"Life is short! Dessert comes first!"

"I'm so sorry, Bridget! I will never try to get between you and your bakery-addiction again."

"See that you don't!" They walked side-by-side toward the Old West town. "Where do we get the four-wheelers from?"

"The stable, which is right beside the café. We're going out of our way for the bakery, but at least we can go straight to the stable from there."

"Does Miranda bake the same things every day? Or does she sometimes get creative?"

Kevin shrugged. "You know, I don't think I'd ever been in the bakery until yesterday. I just never made it there."

Bridget stopped walking. "I…I feel like I don't even *know* you! How could you not go into a bakery? What a strange man you are!"

He laughed, taking her hand in his. "I promise that's the only thing that's odd about me. I mean, I like sweets, I just don't *need* them like some people do."

"Some people meaning me, right?"

He nodded emphatically. "My very own Bridget the Midget."

"You don't get to call me that! You have to call me Bridget the Beautiful. Or Bridget the Brain."

"Bridget the Brain?"

She shrugged. "I was a nursing major. I tutored science."

"I kind of like Bridget the Beautiful. It doesn't have the same ring to it as Bridget the Midget, but I can make do."

"So kind of you." Bridget shook her head. "You're not so great for my ego, you know."

"Why not? I think you're beautiful. I just said that!"

"You think I'm beautiful in a stick me in your pocket and carry me around kind of way. I'm not beautiful and we both know it. I'm cute. That's it."

He laughed. "You're beautiful to me. I think you're pretty darned special."

She spotted the bakery. "Race you to the yummy stuff." She didn't give him any time to prepare and just started running, giving herself a good head start. When she reached the building, she opened the door, completely out of breath and giggling hysterically.

Miranda looked startled for a moment, but then she grinned. "Bridget!"

"Hi, Miranda! I need my yummies for the day."

Kevin walked in behind her, glaring. "You cheated."

"All's fair in desserts and war!"

"Isn't that supposed to be 'love and war?'" His voice was low, and he had a silly grin on his face.

Bridget shook her head. "I don't believe in falling in love in two days. Doesn't happen in my world, so it's in dessert and war."

Kevin smiled, one finger tracing her cheek softly. "You just keep telling yourself that."

Bridget tore her gaze from his and walked to the counter, her face red, and her heart racing. "Let me see what I want today."

It didn't take her long to choose a pineapple upside down cupcake and a cannoli. Once they were wrapped up, and Kevin had paid for them over her protests, they were on their way. "I'll see you tomorrow!" Bridget waved as they walked to the stable.

"Have you ever ridden a four-wheeler?" he asked.

She nodded. "A few times. I'm proficient."

"Okay, good." Once they had their four-wheelers, they drove to the cafe.

He turned to her after they parked on the grass beside the building. "I'll get our lunch."

"I want to come in! I need to see Kelsi!"

Kevin shrugged, carrying the desserts inside with him.

As they walked in, Bridget saw a girl she hadn't met yet talking to Kelsi, who said, "We've been keeping it secret, but I have to tell you or I'm going to burst."

Kelsi's eyes widened and she squealed, hugging the other girl. "Belly bump!" She bumped her belly with the woman in front of her, seeming thrilled to be able to do so. Her gaze met Bridget's, and she smiled. "This is my sister-in-law, Belinda. She's making a cousin for little Herbert here." She patted her belly with a grin.

"Herbert?" Bridget asked, flinching visibly. She wouldn't really name her baby Herbert, would she?

Kelsi grinned. "Well, we just found out it's a girl, so probably not Herbert, but I've been trying out different names for her. Herberta, maybe?"

Bridget shook her head emphatically. "Just keep trying." She smiled at Belinda, who looked embarrassed at the idea of being discussed so openly. "It's nice to meet you. I'm Kaya's sister, Bridget."

Belinda's eyes opened wide and she nodded. "Oh! I'm Wyatt's wife. We got married this summer. Wyatt and Glen work together. I love your sister."

"It's nice to meet you. I'm sure I'll see you at the reception on Saturday."

Belinda nodded. "I wouldn't miss it." She looked back at Kelsi. "I'll see you soon. And I'm not sure how I feel about the whole belly bumping thing."

Kelsi shrugged. "You'll get used to it! The cousins need to get to know one another!"

"Won't that be easier once their out of the wombs?"

"Never too early!"

Belinda shook her head and headed out the door, obviously flustered by her sister-in-law's reaction to her pregnancy.

"We need lunch, Kelsi. To go." Kevin, had his hand at the back of Bridget's waist, and Kelsi smiled knowingly.

"The ranch is bringing another couple together, isn't it? I don't think it's possible to not fall in love here anymore."

Bridget had no idea how to respond to that. "I..."

"Oh, stop pretending you're shy. I know better!"

Bridget sighed. "Where'd you get the idea for the belly bump? I met this crazy woman who ran around yelling 'boobie bump' and then she'd hug you. This is like the same thing for pregnant women!"

Kelsi laughed as she efficiently packed a lunch into a box for the two of them. "I learned it from your sister, and then I modified it to fit my own needs. If Kaya would hurry up and get pregnant, it would suit me very well."

Bridget didn't know how to respond to that. "I think they're going to wait. Glen wants his business more established first."

"I don't blame him, but I still want Kaya to have a baby near the age of mine. Wouldn't that be so much fun?" Kelsi pushed the lunch at Kevin, who paid her at the old-fashioned cash register at the end of the counter.

"I guess? But people can't just have babies to amuse you."

Kelsi shrugged. "If only the world revolved around me."

Bridget shook her head. "We still on for scary movies tonight?"

Kelsi nodded. "Why not? It sounds like fun to me, and the men can amuse themselves somehow."

As much as Bridget wanted more time alone with Kevin, she knew that being around other people would help her know him better. Maybe she'd find some really annoying habit, and her feelings would change. A girl could hope, couldn't she?

Chapter Five

THEY RODE for a full hour before Kevin pulled over to the side of the trail, and Bridget followed him. He took the boxed lunch Kelsi had made for them and moved over to a bench, conveniently placed by the Westons for their guests. He sat down, waiting for Bridget to follow him, admiring the way she moved in her jeans and blue T-shirt. She shouldn't look good with as big as the shirt was on her, but she did. Her shirt read, "Cute enough to stop your heart. Skilled enough to restart it." She had a jacket tied around her waist and knotted at the front.

When she was sitting beside him, he divvied up the food, giving them each a sandwich, a bag of chips, and a bottle of water. "I know it's not gourmet, but it'll have to do."

She opened the bottle of water, tilted her head back, and drained half of it. "I'm not a girl who needs gourmet. Never have been. Spending the day in the wilderness with a halfway decent looking guy is good enough for me."

"Halfway decent? Don't strain yourself coming up with something nice to say now." He wasn't offended exactly, but he was a little surprised she could only come up with halfway decent as a descriptor. He'd been called a lot of things nicer than halfway decent.

She shrugged. "Well, you know. I don't want you to get a big head or anything. Your church is small and you need to fit."

"Always looking out for the needs of others. I appreciate that about you."

"It's true. I think about you before myself." She opened the sandwich to see what was there and smiled. "Pimento cheese and ham. Yum." It was the good kind of pimento cheese too, not the nasty stuff from a jar. She wasn't sure if it was homemade or came in a tub, but it looked and smelled good.

He grinned. "Kelsi keeps pimento cheese stocked for me. It's not super common around here, and I'm probably the only one who orders it."

"Well, it should be common everywhere!" She took a big bite of the sandwich and giggled when she saw he had a bit of cheese below his bottom lip. She reached over and used her thumb to rub it away. "You're wearing your cheese."

"Saving it for later."

She laughed, shaking her head. "Are there any napkins in that box? Cuz I don't want to run around all day with cheese on my face."

"Better to have cheese on your face than egg on your face, right?" he asked as he dug through the box for napkins and handed her a couple. "I love it up here. It's so quiet. I know it's chilly, but the view is worth it. I wish there was a little church up here. It feels like the right place to worship."

"Will it be worth it in the snow?"

He nodded. "Snow brings skiers and snowmobiles. We

have outdoor sports here year-round. Of course, I'm fond of sitting by a fire during the winter." He looked over at her. "It seems like something I should do with someone I love though."

She wouldn't meet his eyes. It was the second time he'd used that word in an hour, and it scared her a little. Was she ready for love? With a *pastor?* "Are you going to the reception on Saturday?" She couldn't deal with that topic just yet.

He nodded. "Glen asked me the last time I had to help out in the stable."

"Are you taking anyone?" What if he'd already made plans to be with another girl? It would break her heart to see him dancing with someone else.

"I was hoping to take you." He took the hand that rested on the bench between them. "You're the only girl I want to take anywhere."

Bridget bit her lip as she looked at him. "I'm afraid feelings are running too high too fast. And I don't know why."

He sighed, his thumb rubbing the palm of her hand. "I think we're meant to be together. There's something special between us."

"But I'm going home to Texas on Monday."

He frowned. "It's only Wednesday. I'll just have to work on convincing you to stay with me."

"I'm not sure that's wise. I'm not really cut out to be a pastor's wife."

"Why not?" He knew she wasn't the type of girl he'd pictured being married to, but she was special, and she was a Christian. What else really mattered?

She shrugged. "Mainly because I can't help but tell people the truth. If someone says, 'Does this make me look fat?' I say, "It's certainly not flattering!' and then they get all offended. My shoes are made of chocolate peppermint, because it's the only way I can stand the taste of the feet that are always in my mouth!"

"You haven't offended me!"

"I haven't said anything that you found odd or off-putting?"

He wanted to say no, but how could he? She did say strange things. "You have. But I don't have a congregation. My job is different than that of most pastors."

"What if you change? What if you decide to do something else, and I end up leading women's Bible studies? When I was a kid, they wouldn't let me ask questions during Sunday school, because I kept offending the teachers. Finally, they had to have someone sit with me at all times. Same thing during youth group, but that was because I was a flight risk."

He bit back a laugh. "Flight risk?"

"One little trip to a convenience store when I was supposed to be at youth group, and there was an adult stationed at the door every day until I graduated."

Kevin shook his head. "I think I love you, Bridget the Midget."

Bridget sighed heavily. "I thought you were going to call me something else."

He leaned down and kissed her softly. "I like Bridget the Midget, and I say it with all the love inside me. Please promise you'll think about staying in Idaho."

"Not a chance." She might come back though. She couldn't stay, because she had to be back at work on Tuesday. There were people who depended on her.

"Then spend as much time with me as you can while you're here." He felt like he was acting like a stray dog, begging her for scraps, but he didn't care. Pride was a sin, so he didn't need to keep any.

She nodded slowly, leaning toward him for another kiss. "I promise."

He took a deep breath, trying to control the emotions flooding through him. "Are you finished? This is supposed to be a good spot to hunt for Bigfoot."

"Yeah. What are we doing tomorrow?"

He frowned. "I have to work in the general store for six hours tomorrow. Maybe we can spend the evening together."

"Doing what?"

"I'll probably be manning the cash register. Heidi prefers to be helping people herself."

Bridget thought he'd lost his mind for a moment before she realized he was answering the wrong question. "I was asking what you want to do tomorrow."

He shrugged. "You decide."

"I'll think about it."

As they looked for Bigfoot clues, she asked him the question that she always asked. "Cindy or Belle?"

"I haven't decided yet. Does it matter so much?"

Bridget nodded emphatically. "Of course it matters! I need an answer soon!"

"Maybe we should watch some more Disney movies. If I had a better picture in my head of the different princesses, maybe I could choose one."

"You're just being persnickety! If you choose Ariel or Jasmine, I'm going to have something to say!"

"Isn't there a new princess in town? Something about an ice queen or something?"

"Elsa? She was a couple of years ago. There's a new princess movie coming out at the end of this month. *Moana*, I think it's called. I can't wait to see it."

"If you come back, I'll take you to see it."

She sighed. "Maybe we should watch *The Little*

Mermaid, *Aladdin*, and *Frozen* instead." She stooped down to see if the broken branch she spotted was a sign of Bigfoot. "Do you think Kelsi would change plans? I think we're going to need to Disney all week if we're going to get through the princesses so you can decide for yourself."

"I think she'd be amenable to that."

"Do you have her number? I want to call!"

He nodded, pulling his phone from his pocket and flipping through his contacts. He handed it to her when he'd found the right one. He was surprised she didn't want to text, but maybe she was old school.

She pressed the button to call and waited impatiently for Kelsi to answer.

"Hello?"

"Kelsi, were you sleeping?"

"Yeah, I'm sleeping for two." There was a loud yawn from the other end of the connection.

"Can we watch some Disney princess movies tonight instead of horror flicks?"

"You're trying to convince Kevin that Cindy's better than Belle still, aren't you? Give it up!"

"So what if I am?"

Kelsi sighed. "Yeah, has he seen *Cinderella* and *Beauty and the Beast* yet?"

"Yeah, we watched those last night. Time to move on to *Frozen*, *Aladdin*, *The Little Mermaid*, *The Frog Prince*, *Sleeping Beauty*, *Snow White*…"

"Was he raised in a barn? He doesn't know any of the princess movies?"

"Nope."

"Fine. I have *Aladdin* and *Frozen*. Will those work?"

"Perfectly. Can I bring anything?"

"Your body and your appetite. Seven. We'll eat in front

of the princesses. He's going to do the right thing and choose Belle."

Bridget could only laugh when she realized the call had ended. "We're watching Elsa and Jasmine tonight."

"I don't know who they are, and I'm afraid to ask. I guess I'll find out when I get there."

She turned to him, looping her arms around his neck. "I think you're pretty terrific, even though you are a pastor." She stood on tiptoe to press her lips to his, wishing she was just a little taller so she could reach him better.

He caught her by the waist, holding her close as he returned the kiss. "I wish that didn't count against me."

She rested her forehead against his shoulder. "I wish it didn't too."

Burying his face in her hair, he held her for just a moment. "Your hair smells like oranges."

She smiled. "Citrus shampoo."

"I like it." He sighed. "It's probably time for us to head back. It's a little after three, but it gets dark early this time of year."

She nodded, not ready to move away from him. "I could stand here like this forever."

"Or until your flight leaves on Monday." He didn't want to think about her leaving. He wanted to put her in his pocket and keep her there forever. She was so tiny, she just might fit. It was hard to believe she and Kaya were twins.

"I'm not ready to think about leaving. I'm going to concentrate on standing here with you." *And loving you.* She couldn't admit it aloud yet, but she knew it was true. She was in love with a pastor who lived in Idaho. What was the world coming to?

* * *

After her nap, Bridget got dressed and fixed her hair. She always thought of it as mouse brown. She brushed it out and added a few curls with a curling iron. She wanted to look her best. They only had five more evenings together before she flew back to Texas. They wouldn't even have the day together on Thursday. She would miss him, but she looked forward to the chance to explore the ranch on her own.

She was waiting on the couch when he got there. Her parents had once again disappeared to go off and dance somewhere. She was just glad she didn't have to watch them!

When the knock came at the door, she shrugged into her coat and hurried to open it. Kevin stepped inside, surprising her. A quick kiss had her mumbling something incoherent about tingling, but she quickly regained her composure. "We'd better hurry. No telling what Kelsi will do if we're late!" She grabbed his hand and tugged him toward the door, locking it behind them.

Once they were in the car, he glanced over at her. "So we're doing what movies tonight?"

"Jasmine and Elsa. *Aladdin* and *Frozen*. I'm not fond of Jasmine. She's a whiny princess. I like Elsa, because she has this whole girl power thing going on. You'll see."

"I think Belle was kind of girl power too. At least she was a lot more so than Cinderella."

"Are you leaning toward Belle?" Bridget asked in shock. "You are, aren't you?"

"I can't say until I've seen more of the movies. How can I possibly make an informed decision about something so important to you?"

Bridget glared at him, before turning her head to look out the window at the darkness. "Doesn't Kelsi live on the ranch?"

"Nope. She lives in town with her husband, the sheriff."

"That's cool, I guess. I can't really see Kelsi married to law enforcement."

"From what I hear, he has been in love with her for years, and when her worthless ex-boyfriend moved to California hoping to be a Disney prince, Shane asked her out that very day. They married a week later or something ridiculous like that."

"You think quick marriages are ridiculous?"

"Not at all. I'd marry you tomorrow."

She sighed. "You're not going to let it go, are you?" After he saw *Frozen*, she'd be able to sing the song to him. Incessantly.

"How could I?"

The houses were getting closer together, and there were some streetlights, which told her they were in town. "How big is Riston?" Her sister had talked about the nearest town a lot.

"I have no idea. Small. There's a grocery store and a few other businesses. You can get everything you *need* here, but you can't necessarily get what you want. You have to go into a bigger city for that."

"Thank God for Amazon then, right?"

He laughed. "I guess so." He pulled into a driveway, and they got out, walking to the door together.

A man she hadn't met yet came to the door. "You must be Bridget. I'm Shane, Kelsi's husband."

"Don't let her name the baby Herberta!"

Shane shook his head, laughing. "I'm not letting her name the baby Herberta or anything else weird!" He turned and raised his voice. "You hear me, Kelsi? No Herberta!"

"I'm carrying this baby! I get to name her!" Kelsi came

out of the kitchen, drying her hands on a dish towel. "Come in! Come in! Enchiladas are ready. I made a pan and a half of mild and half a pan of good."

Shane sighed. "By good she means so hot it'll burn a hole in your tongue."

Bridget walked into the house, shrugging her coat off. "You can eat spicy things while you're pregnant?" she asked with surprise. "Most women can't!"

Kelsi shrugged. "It doesn't bother me so far. Doctor said I have to lay off my Cajun seasoning, because it's messing with my blood pressure though. What does he know?"

Shane patted Kelsi's shoulder. "You'll get through it. You can start having it again as soon as she's born."

"You bet your sweet little patootie I can!" Kelsi took Bridget's coat from her.

"Do you need help with anything?" Bridget asked, following behind Kelsi down a hallway to her bedroom, and watching her throw the coat on her bed.

"Nah. It's all done. Just need to serve it."

Fifteen minutes later, they were on the couch together, while the two men sat in chairs, talking softly. "Jasmine first?" Kelsi asked.

"Definitely!" Bridget said. "I don't think Kevin will like Jasmine as much as Elsa."

"I guess we're about to find out." Kelsi pushed the button and started the show, then took a bite of her enchiladas. "Do you want a bite? Kaya is the only person I know who matches my love for crazy spicy stuff."

"No thank you! Kaya's taste buds were burned off when we were little. Keep that stuff away from me." Bridget cut off a bite of her enchilada with the side of her fork, before popping a bite into her mouth. She immediately coughed and reached for water. "This is mild?"

"Oh yeah. It's mild." Kelsi took a bite of hers. "Are you sure you don't want to try the good stuff?"

Bridget's eyes were wide as she shook her head. "No. I can barely handle this!"

"No hot sauce then?"

Bridget shook her head, looking at Kevin who was biting his lip to keep from laughing. She glared at him as the movie started, and then she settled back to watch it. She couldn't wait!

When it came time for the songs, she did her best not to sing as loudly as usual. She didn't want Kelsi and Shane to think badly of her.

When they left the other couple's house that night, Bridget asked Kevin what he'd thought. "See? Neither is as good as Cindy or Belle."

"I don't know. I liked Elsa and Anna a lot. Anna was such a spunky little thing. For a bit, it seemed like Elsa was going to be the villain of the show, but that prince was a real treat, wasn't he?"

Bridget shook her head. "I hate Prince Hans. He was horrid. I always wonder if Anna will get to marry Christophe. With it being a Disney movie, you'd think so, but they don't tell you! All the princesses marry at the end!"

"Does it bother you that they didn't marry?"

She shrugged. "Maybe. I wanted to see her marry a commoner. I think it would have been good for her. Elsa though…how are they ever going to get someone to marry the Ice Queen?"

When they reached the Bearfoot Bungalow, she put her hand on the door handle, but he stopped her. "Wait for just a minute."

She turned toward him in the seat. "Why?"

He put his hands on her shoulders and pulled her to

him. "So I can do this." His lips settled on hers, and his hands stroked up and down her arms. "I hate that we don't get to spend tomorrow together. What will you do?"

"I'll wander around the ranch on my own, explore everything. Maybe I'll talk Kaya into coming with me, but probably not. I like the idea of wandering around thinking." She planned to seek out Wade for a shot at the nursing post, but she didn't tell him that. She didn't want him to get his hopes up, when she wasn't sure if she even wanted to stay. Well, that wasn't true. She knew she wanted to stay. She just didn't know if she would get a position that would allow her to stay.

"I'll get off around six. So we could do the next round of movies at seven? I'd love to take you to the restaurant if you want."

She shook her head. "Maybe Sunday night, before I leave. I want to get through as many of the princess movies as we can. I'm still waiting for you to make a decision."

He sighed. "I'll try."

She put her hands on his shoulders and kissed his cheek. "I'll miss you tomorrow, but I promise to stay out of trouble if I can."

"If you can? What kind of promise is that?"

"Hey, I don't make promises that I can't keep. Best I can do."

"You've lost it!"

"I never had it. Haven't you realized that yet?" She glanced at the cabin and saw her mother peering out the curtains at her. "Mom's getting worried. I'd better get in there."

"Why is she worried?"

Bridget grinned. "She's worried both of her girls are going to move to Idaho, and there will be no grandbabies close enough for her to love on."

Kevin walked her to the door, kissing her softly. “I'll be here around seven.”

“I'll be waiting.” She went in and closed the door behind her, closing her eyes. Every minute she spent with him, she fell deeper and deeper in love.

Her mother was waiting. “Did you have a good time?”

Bridget nodded, going into the living room and sitting beside her. “We went to Kelsi's and watched a couple of Disney movies.”

“Of course you did. Has he chosen yet?”

“Nope. He will soon.”

“Do you love him?”

Bridget closed her eyes. “Can you really love someone you've known for two days?”

“I knew the instant I met your father he was the man for me.”

“Yeah. I love him. I don't want to, but I do.”

“What are you going to do about it?” Mom asked.

Bridget shrugged. “He's not picking me up until seven tomorrow evening, so I'm going to wander around and think tomorrow. I'm looking forward to exploring the ranch a little on my own.”

“Why isn't he picking you up until late?” Her mom looked at her with concern, and Bridget immediately knew what she was thinking. What everyone who knew her would think. That she'd done something to offend him or someone else, and he was going to stop seeing her. She hated that no one believed anything she said.

“He's working at the general store tomorrow. He fills in for people who need to be out for whatever reason.” Bridget paused for a minute. “I'm thinking about talking to Wade, the ranch manager, about working here as a nurse.”

“I know you are.”

“You do?”

Her mom nodded. "I knew as soon as I heard there was an opening. You're not meant to live so far from your sister, and now that you're in love, it's the place you need to be."

"What about grandbabies?"

Mom sighed. "I guess I'll have to live with the fact that they're here. There's no law saying we can't visit often…or that we can't even move here. We'll make it work. You need to be where you're happy."

Bridget sighed. "Thanks, Mom."

Chapter Six

BRIDGET'S PARENTS were gone when she woke the next morning. It was just after ten, and she was ready to face her day. There was a note waiting for her on the counter. "I made you a lunch. I hope you enjoy your day. Love, Mom."

Bridget grinned at the lunch box in the fridge beside two water bottles. She'd pick up her dessert from the bakery, and wander the ranch. She also needed to find Wade, and she wasn't sure where he worked. He seemed to appear everywhere at different times. Did the man even have an office?

She locked the door and walked off toward the Old West town, deciding she needed to start with finding her dessert. How would she have the energy to make it through the day otherwise? Her blood sugar might drop!

When she opened the door to the bakery, Miranda grinned at her. "You're later than usual today. I was starting to think you weren't coming."

"Not having dessert? Do you not know me at all? I thought we were lifelong friends!"

Miranda laughed. "Of course, we are! Which desserts are you choosing today?"

Ten minutes later, she was off to explore the ranch. She knew there was a lake off to the north somewhere, and she was determined to eat her lunch beside it. She'd worn a hoodie and jeans, because the day before she'd gotten too hot, and then too cold, and then too hot. Between her T-shirt and heavy coat, it was hard to know which was right for the weather, but she'd unearthed her hoodie from the bottom of her suitcase, and it should be just fine.

The hoodie read, "I'm 99.9% sure I'm a Disney Princess." She couldn't help but let her Disney show wherever she went.

As she wandered through the old town, toward the north and the lake she knew was hiding there, she passed a small house with a huge number of gnomes, fairies, and leprechauns guarding it. She stopped and grinned, loving the way it looked. She could live there happily.

She was still looking at the variety of creatures, all grouped together into little villages, when she noticed a bunny stop right in front of her, looking at her. It looked perfectly at home amidst the fun creatures, and Bridget smiled. "You look like you could turn into a fairy any second."

"Oh, the bunnies don't turn into fairies," said a voice with a slight Irish lilt. "The bunnies don't even like the fairies, though I don't know why. Who wouldn't like a fairy?"

"I'm sure I don't know!" Bridget said with a grin. "I'm Bridget Taylor."

"Bridget the Midget! You're Kaya's sister. Come in. I've been expecting you. The fairies told me you'd be along shortly before noon, and here you are. I have tea and snickerdoodles ready. Unless you'd rather have milk, like your sister?"

"I'm not really a milk drinker. Tea would be fine." Bridget followed the older woman into her home. If she knew Kaya, she had to be safe, right?

Sure enough, there was a flowered teapot in the middle of the coffee table, and there was a plate of cookies right beside it. Bridget looked for a place to sit, but they were all covered with bunnies, so she finally scooped one up and put it on her lap. "What's your name?"

The older woman shook her head. "The bunnies don't talk. Only the fairies do. Do you have difficulties telling the difference between bunnies and fairies? I don't remember your sister being quite so difficult."

Bridget grinned, wanting to adopt the old woman as her grandmother on the spot. "May I call you Grandma?"

"Why would you want to do that? My name is Jaclyn—Jaclyn Hardy. No need to call me anything else."

"It's very nice to meet you, Jaclyn." In her head she'd call her Grandma. Who could stop her?

Jaclyn poured them each a cup of tea, and then she put a couple of cookies onto a plate and handed them to Bridget. "That should satisfy your sweet tooth for at least a minute or two."

"Did the fairies tell you I like sweet things?" Bridget asked, fascinated by the conversation.

Jaclyn's eyebrow rose. "You're carrying a bakery bag. I can add two and two without coming up with five."

Bridget looked at the bag in her hand and giggled. "I guess I was carried away by the magic of your home."

Jaclyn sat back and smiled, raising her tea cup to her lips. "It is rather magical here, isn't it?"

"Oh, yes. I love it! Will you be at my sister's wedding reception on Saturday?"

"Of course, I will. The fairies and I worked hard to bring Kaya and Glen together. We wouldn't miss their reception for anything!"

"I didn't know the fairies helped with Kaya and Glen. My sister must have forgotten to mention that. Tell me about the fairies." Bridget couldn't express just how utterly delighted she was by the older woman. If she'd told her it was time for her to move into a cave at the bottom of the lake, she would have happily gone spelunking.

"No one gives the fairies any credit for the matches they painstakingly make, but they should!"

"Do the gnomes ever help make matches?"

"Of course not! The gnomes are altogether too stuck-up for that nonsense. No, the gnomes won't even speak to me." Jaclyn sighed heavily. "Of course, that may have something to do with me killing poor George. I didn't mean to hurt him."

"Oh, no! What happened to poor George?"

"I thought I heard a prowler and I killed him with my garden rake. It wasn't my intention, of course, but the other gnomes have just never forgiven me."

"I'm so sorry." Bridget reached over and placed her hand over Jaclyn's, dislodging the bunny in the process.

"Are you making fun of me?" Jaclyn asked, her face skeptical.

"No! I wouldn't ever make fun of you!" Bridget had learned to humor older people who had dementia, but she didn't think that was the case with Jaclyn. No, Jaclyn seemed to have her full faculties.

"All right. Well, I'm sure you're wondering why the fairies and I invited you for tea."

Bridget didn't mention the fact that she hadn't gotten an invitation for fear she'd offend the other woman. "I am *very* curious."

"Well, it's about you and the pastor. He's a good man. Did you know he's been in this area since he graduated from high school? People tend to think he's a local, but you'd think that Texas twang would give him away. I don't know why it doesn't actually..." Jaclyn got a far-away look in her eyes, and Bridget wondered if she'd forgotten she was there. After a moment, she looked back at her. "Oh, right. Well, you and Pastor Kevin are going to need a little prodding from the fairies to get things right."

"We are? Do you think we should get things right? I'm not exactly pastor's wife material."

"I don't know why not! You're a good woman, Bridget Taylor. You're a bit odd, and that's a fact, but who isn't? I want you to go seek out Wade today and apply for that nursing post."

Bridget bit her lip. "I was planning on it last night, but in the light of day, I couldn't help but wonder if it was a mistake. I'm not Cinderella after all, and he's not my Prince Charming, ready to rescue me."

"Do you need Prince Charming to rescue you? Despite what your shirt says, I don't think you believe you're a Disney princess."

"No, I don't. I wouldn't mind being one, though."

"Are you sure about that? You've worked really hard to get where you are in life. If you were a princess, you wouldn't be able to work at all. No, I think you want to be Bridget with a man who treats you with respect. Just like Pastor Kevin does."

Bridget pursed her lips. "You might be right."

"You go and think about it." Jaclyn stood up and plucked the tea cup out of Bridget's hand.

Bridget was barely able to save her cookies before her plate was taken as well. When the bunny was removed from her lap, she knew the older woman meant business.

"I'm going! Would you tell me if I'm walking in the right direction to reach the lake?"

Jaclyn nodded. "Yes, keep walking north. You're only a few minutes away at a brisk pace. Enjoy the butterflies."

Bridget was on the porch and the door was slammed in her face before she could ask about butterflies. It was November in Idaho. Surely there were no butterflies around!

She continued her walk, her mind on the conversation with the eccentric woman. Was she really meant to be with Kevin? And have a life there?

She found the lake a few minutes later, and sat down at a picnic table. She was the only one in the covered picnic area, and she rubbed her arms against the chill. It smelled like snow! She didn't know how she'd picked it up with as seldom as it snowed in Texas, but one of her college roommates had claimed to be able to smell snow. Bridget had scoffed, but sure enough, she'd predicted snow when the weatherman hadn't, right before it started falling.

And Bridget had remembered the smell very well. The last two times it had snowed she'd known it was coming. Because of the smell. She should have worn her heavy jacket after all.

She opened the lunch box her mother had packed and pulled out the sandwich there, before bursting out laughing. Her sandwich had been cut into the shape of two butterflies. Surely, she would enjoy them. Jaclyn was a mystery, but she was one Bridget hoped she'd never solve. Who wanted to understand the magic?

After lunch, she wandered toward the main house on the ranch, hoping someone there could point her in the direction of Wade. She really wanted to talk to him about the nursing position there on the ranch. She would take a cut in pay if it meant she could live in the little nurse's apartment above the apothecary shop.

A man waved her down from a distance. "You need to be wearing a heavier coat!" he called.

Bridget squinted her eyes, and she hurried toward him. "Wade Weston, right?"

The man nodded, his ice blue eyes narrowed. "Yes, I'm Wade. We met the other day in the general store, right? You were with Pastor Kevin."

"Yes. I'm Kaya's sister. I was wondering if you had a minute to talk to me."

"Has there been a problem with the ranch?" Wade oversaw everyone, and usually guest service complaints ended up on his desk at some point, but it wasn't often he was the first point of contact.

"No. There's no problem. I'm a nurse, you see, and I was wondering how to apply for Emily's position. She told me she's retiring."

Wade tilted his head to one side as if studying her carefully. "It's starting to snow. Why don't we go sit in the café and talk? We can have some hot coffee and warm up a bit. Which cabin are you in?"

"The Bearfoot! I love that name, by the way." She fell into step beside him, happy that he was willing to take a few minutes with her.

Wade sighed. "It's tolerable." He turned and led the way to the café, his long strides eating up the distance, while Bridget half ran to keep up with him.

"My legs are short!" she protested finally.

He glanced back at her. "I guess they are." He opened the door to the café and led her to a booth off to one side.

Kelsi was there right away to get their orders. "Hi, Bridget! Hey, big brother. What are you eating today?"

"Hot coffee for both of us," Wade said. He looked at Bridget with a frown. "You *do* drink coffee, don't you?"

Bridget nodded. "I do. A slice of pie would be nice too."

Wade raised an eyebrow. "Get me one too. What's the pie today?"

"Mississippi Mud."

"Oh, yum!" Bridget smiled happily. She'd eaten the cookies with her lunch, but she'd be able to save the desserts from the bakery for dinner. Sugar should be its own food group!

Wade turned his attention to her. "You have an accent that tells me you're not from around here."

"Texas. I'm a nurse for a family practice in North Texas."

"What makes you think you want to live in Idaho?"

As she answered each of his questions, Bridget couldn't help but think about how no-nonsense the man was. If she hadn't been impressed when she'd met him before, she certainly was now. He wasn't taking note of anything she said, but the look in his eyes told her he wouldn't forget.

After they'd had their coffee and pie, she reached into her pocket for her share of the bill, but he held up a hand. "No, this is on the ranch. Make sure you stop by the front desk in the bunk house before you leave. If everything checks out, you have yourself a job. Do you know if your nursing license will transfer?"

"I actually looked that up last night. It doesn't look like a difficult process, and I can get an immediate temporary license. I will need to give two weeks' notice to my current job, so it'll be after Thanksgiving before I can start."

Wade nodded. "That will work. Emily will need to stay on for a short while to train you as well."

Bridget frowned. "I guess I can stay with my sister during that time."

"We can get you a room on the ranch if we need to."

She nodded. She didn't want to put the ranch out, but living with newlyweds when she didn't really get along with her sister to begin with was not her idea of a good idea. "I'll fill out an application now."

"I'd appreciate that." He stood and shook her hand. "Welcome to the team."

Bridget hurried to the bunk house, which she knew was the name that had been given to the building with most of the guestrooms. She asked for an application and filled it out quickly before walking casually back to the cabin for her nap. Her heart was pounding with excitement, and not just because of the thin layer of snow that was sticking to the ground along the path, transforming the already beautiful ranch into a winter wonderland.

She had made the first step toward moving to Idaho and changing her life. She wouldn't tell Kevin until she knew for sure though. She didn't want to get his hopes up. Or her own.

* * *

That evening, when Kevin picked Bridget up, she wore her heavy coat and gloves over her hoodie. Once they were in the car, she turned to him. "I need to buy a gnome. Where can I buy a gnome?"

He frowned, shrugging. "I have no idea. Why do you need to buy a gnome?"

"Because Jaclyn killed George with her garden rake."

Kevin blinked a few times, doing his best to make sense of what she'd said. "I don't know what that means."

"You don't need to! Can you take me somewhere we can get a gnome tomorrow? I want to take it to Jaclyn."

He frowned. "I like Jaclyn, but she's a bit odd. Why do you want to take her a gnome again?"

Bridget sighed. "Because she killed George with her rake. That's the only explanation you're getting from me."

Finally he shrugged. "Sure, we'll drive into Lewiston tomorrow, and we'll buy a gnome."

"Thank you."

Kevin had no idea what any of it meant, but if it would make her happy, he was willing to do it. She meant a lot to him after all. "I picked up some burgers and onion rings in town for supper. Will that work? They won't be as good as Bob's burgers, but at least they'll be something to eat."

Bridget shrugged. "Sounds good. I have dessert with me too."

"You didn't eat it earlier?"

"No, Jaclyn gave me snickerdoodles, and I had a piece of Mississippi Mud pie at the café. Even I can't eat two desserts on top of that in a two-hour period."

"I guess you enjoyed your day?" He pulled up in front of the main house, and they went to the library where they'd watched movies on Tuesday night. "What are we watching tonight, anyway?"

"*The Little Mermaid* and *Brave* are on the agenda. I called and made sure they were in the library before you got to the cabin."

He frowned. "I may have seen *The Little Mermaid*. Wasn't there a big octopus witch thing?"

"Yeah, she's the Sea Hag." Bridget found the movies while he divvied up their food and sat down right smack in the middle of the couch. When she saw where he was sitting, she laughed. "Trying to make sure we're close enough to snuggle?"

"It's a cold night!" He pushed a button on a remote she hadn't noticed before, and an electric fire sprang to life. "There's a real fire place in the main room, but since this room is used mostly by guests, the ranch plays it safe."

Bridget popped the first movie in before walking over and sinking onto the couch beside him. She picked up her burger and took a big bite. He was right. It was edible, but it certainly wasn't as good as Bob's.

She had chosen *Brave* to be the first movie, knowing he wouldn't have seen it. It was too new. He would have been in college when it first came out, and going to Disney movies was not the typical pastime of most college guys.

She realized she'd forgotten forks, so she pulled two Belle forks from her purse, handing him one. He looked at it for a moment before shaking his head. "I can't believe I'm watching Disney movies while eating with a princess shrimp fork. You've turned my life upside down, and I've only known you three days!"

"I work fast," she said, popping a bite of cake into her mouth. "Miranda's a genius."

He just grinned, waiting while she popped in the second movie. He hadn't been overly fond of Brave, but it hadn't been terrible. It was certainly better than the ones where the princesses sat around waiting to be rescued.

For the second movie, she snuggled closely against him, his arm around her, and her head pillowed on his shoulder. She could get used to having a man around to snuggle with.

After the second movie ended, she turned to him. "So? Cindy or Belle?"

He shrugged. "I can't make up my mind."

She sighed. "You're really going to be difficult about this, aren't you?"

"I promise to make my decision before Monday."

She rested her forehead against his shoulder. "I can't believe you're making me wait until the last minute. That's just cruel!"

"It means more nights spent watching movies with you and cuddling on this couch."

She brushed her lips against his. "You sure know the way to a woman's heart…"

"Disney movies?" he asked, raising an eyebrow.

"What else?"

Chapter Seven

By noon the following morning, Kevin was at the wheel driving Bridget back to the ranch, a small gnome in the backseat. "What movies are we watching tonight?" he asked.

She frowned. "I was thinking *Pocahontas* and *Tangled*. We still have so many we haven't gotten to. You're still going to make your decision before Monday, though, right?"

He nodded. "I promise I will." He actually had something in mind, and he would spend most of the day on it before the reception the following day. "I'll be working on something most of the day tomorrow. Are you spending the day with your family?"

Bridget nodded. "I was hoping to spend the day with you, but Kaya texted, and she wants the three of us to have massages and then hair appointments together. And pedicures. I'll be in appointments right up until it's time to get ready for the reception."

Kevin smiled, happy that Kaya had gone along with his plan. He'd make it work somehow. Having an ally in his corner would help tremendously. "I'll miss you, but I understand."

"You'll have to go to the bakery and get four desserts for me if you can."

"I'll find a way." Saturday would be busy, but she was worth it.

He parked behind the main house on the ranch, and walked around to get the gnome from the back seat. "Are we going to the café first or to see Jaclyn?"

"Oh, Jaclyn first. I'm sure the fairies told her to expect us."

Kevin sighed. "I haven't spent a lot of time talking to Jaclyn, but you don't think she really talks to fairies, do you?"

Bridget shrugged, taking the hand he offered. "Well, I don't know. I believe she thinks she talks to fairies, and that's good enough for me. I like her. I want to adopt her as my grandmother, but she said I can't call her grandma."

"Why not?"

"No idea. Something about Jaclyn being her name and I needed to use it. No skin off my nose. I'll just call her Grandma in my head where no one can hear me."

They walked while they talked, and they soon found themselves at Jaclyn's house. Bridget frowned as they got to the yard. "I should have wrapped the gnome."

"She's not expecting a gift! I'm sure it's fine that you didn't wrap it."

"I hope it is. I feel like I should have. It's always awkward just handing someone a bag."

"Jaclyn doesn't strike me as the overly formal type." Kevin raised his hand to knock on the door just as it opened.

"Come in! Come in! We were expecting you!"

"We?" Kevin asked, even as he told himself not to. The words just sneaked past his lips.

"The bunnies, fairies, and I." Jaclyn held the door wide, and sure enough, Bridget saw the teapot, three cups, and three plates on the table. "Have a seat."

Bridget happily scooped up a bunny from the couch and held it so she could sit down. She was always amazed by how very soft rabbits were. "I brought you something."

Jaclyn looked startled for a moment. "You did? It's not my birthday!"

"Didn't the fairies tell you I was bringing a gift?"

Jaclyn shook her head. "Sometimes they like me to be surprised. The stinkers."

Kevin held up the bag containing the gnome, and Jaclyn opened it, peering inside. She pulled it from the bag and turned it over in her hands. When she looked at Bridget again, there were tears in her eyes. "To replace George?"

"No. I get the feeling nothing can replace George. To help you heal from his loss."

Jaclyn swiped away a tear. "Thank you. That's very kind. I think I'll call him Gorgeous George to distinguish him from the original George. That should appease the gnomes." She set the gnome on the floor, where three bunnies hopped to investigate their new friend.

Jaclyn poured three cups of tea, handing one to each of them. "It's good of you to finally visit me, Pastor Kevin. I was beginning to think you were avoiding me."

Kevin flushed, shaking his head. "Of course not. I just wasn't sure when a good time was."

"It's always a good time for a handsome young man to visit me. I'm an old lady, and I have to get my thrills somewhere." Jaclyn handed each of the others a plate of cookies. "How are the Disney movies coming along? Have you made your decision yet?"

Kevin shook his head, assuming Bridget must have mentioned all the movies they were watching when she visited the previous day. "I haven't yet. I promised I'd make a decision by Monday, though."

"Well, if you need a fairy godmother to help you along with your plans, I certainly fit the bill." She laughed uproariously at her own joke.

Bridget frowned. "What does that mean?"

Kevin shrugged, wondering how the older woman knew what he was planning. He hadn't told anyone, not even when he'd called Kaya to have her get Bridget out of the way. "Are you going to be attending the reception tomorrow evening?" he asked.

Jaclyn nodded. "I always attend the weddings and receptions of the couples the fairies and I help along. I don't think they'd forgive me if I didn't."

"I'm sure Glen and Kaya would forgive you!" Kevin protested.

"Oh, Glen and Kaya would definitely forgive me. It's the fairies I'm talking about. They like me to return home and give them all the details about the celebration. It makes them happy."

"Do you dance, Jaclyn?"

Jaclyn shrugged. "Depends on the music, now doesn't it? I wouldn't dance a Texas two-step, but an Irish jig? Or an Irish clog dance would have me stomping my feet with the best of them."

Bridget's lips twitched. "So if I ask you to dance with me tomorrow, I need to do it during an Irish dance?"

Jaclyn shook her head. "I only dance with handsome men, so don't bother. Now if the pastor asked me to dance..."

Bridget nudged Kevin with her elbow. "You hear that? Jaclyn wants to dance with you. You're not going to be stuck dancing with just me."

Kevin blushed, shaking his head. He didn't mind being the center of attention, but not this kind of attention. "I'm not the best dancer. That's not exactly something they teach you at seminary."

"You're still dancing with me. Don't even try to get out of it!"

Kevin sighed. "I guess I'm not going to get out of it, am I?"

Jaclyn smiled at the young couple. "You two are going to make it work. I just know it."

Bridget frowned looking down at her hands. She wanted to agree with the older woman so much, but she was still afraid. What if she wasn't good enough to be a pastor's wife? She didn't want to embarrass him.

Kevin nodded emphatically. "I know we are. We're meant to be together."

Jaclyn stood up. "All right. Thank you for coming."

Bridget took her cookies from her plate to keep them from being taken, but instead, Jaclyn just opened the door and waited for them to go. "I'll see you both tomorrow. Eat those cookies, Bridget. You don't want your blood sugar to drop." As she said it, she threw her head back and laughed.

Kevin looked at Bridget once the door was closed. "Why was that funny?"

She shrugged. "I think she knows that there's some blood in my sugar stream instead of sugar in my blood stream. Anyway, let's go get lunch. I wonder what Bob has on special today."

They walked across the ranch, and Bridget avoided the subject of her relationship with Kevin. "So which princess are you leaning toward? You know Cindy is the best, right?"

Kevin just shook his head. "I refuse to discuss this today. I haven't been able to make a fully informed decision yet. When I do, I will let you know!"

They found a booth and sank into it, a waitress Bridget didn't know came over to take their order. Bridget looked around. "Where's Kelsi?"

"She had an appointment with her obstetrician today."

"I hope she and little Herberta are doing okay."

"Oh yeah. Just a routine visit, I think. I'm Joni. What can I get for you?"

Bridget frowned. There was nothing precisely wrong with the way Joni was taking their order, but it was different than Kelsi. "What's the special today?"

"It's a thick beef noodle soup served with a BLT on rye toast."

Bridget nodded. "That sounds great. Can I get mine without the L and T and with a piece of American cheese?"

Joni nodded, making a note. "You?" she asked Kevin.

"I want the same, but everything on my sandwich and add American cheese. Oh, and we need an order of Bob's fried cheese curds to share."

"To drink?"

"Water," Bridget said.

Kevin nodded. "Water sounds good." As Joni walked away to put their order in, Kevin took her hand in his.

"Every time you do that, I worry that we're announcing our engagement."

"Every time I do what? I haven't officially asked you to marry me yet, so we can't be engaged."

"When you hold my hand. Are pastors allowed to do that in public if they're not engaged?"

Kevin shrugged. "This pastor does it with the woman he loves. I see nothing wrong with it." He looked at her quizzically. "Do you?"

"Oh, not at all. Just making sure we're on the same page."

"We are. About that." He sat back as Joni brought their drinks.

Bridget smiled and thanked her before looking at Kevin again. "Kaya is having me wear a fancy bridesmaid dress tomorrow as if she was actually having her wedding. And the whole day will be spent preparing for this thing. Seems odd since they're already married, but whatever."

"Glen's a good guy. I'm sure he's doing whatever it takes to make Kaya happy. She skipped the big wedding, so she gets to have her reception how she wants it."

"Yeah. She said they were doing it as cheaply as possible as well. Glen's saving every dime for his business."

"Oh, the equestrian therapy thing, right? For autistic kids?"

Bridget nodded. "Does everyone here know he's going to do that?"

"Yup. He talks about it a lot. I don't think it was in his plans yet to marry, but I don't think he regrets it at all. He seems to really love your sister."

"Yeah, and she loves him. I've honestly never been around a couple quite like them. They're lovey-dovey all the time. Kaya and Glen have something special."

"They do." Kevin shrugged. "Some say that the ranch fosters that. There's something in the air or the water or whatever. I don't know. I think things are just real here. It's back to nature. No night clubs. Most people aren't hanging out in bars drinking. They're being real."

"Do you drink?" Bridget asked. She hadn't considered

whether or not he would as a pastor until just that moment.

"No, I don't. I don't think there's anything wrong with an occasional drink as long as someone doesn't get drunk, but as a pastor, I don't want people to get the wrong idea, so I just don't do it. You?"

Bridget shook her head. "Nope. Never have. Never liked the taste, and never saw a need to develop a taste for something that wasn't good for me."

Their food was set on the table in front of them, and Bridget looked inside her sandwich to make sure it was done right. "Thank you. Tell Bob we appreciate his brilliance."

Joni laughed. "Bob's head is big enough already. I'll tell him that you're happy with the food, though."

Bridget looked toward the kitchen. "Hey, Bob! Joni said you have a big head!"

Bob stuck his head out of the kitchen, and Bridget caught sight of him for the first time. "Joni needs to keep her big nose out of my big headedness."

Joni rolled her eyes as she walked away, calling over her shoulder, "Let me know if you need anything."

Kevin shook his head. "You like causing trouble, don't you?"

Bridget shrugged. "Sometimes I do."

"What are you doing this afternoon?" he asked. It had just occurred to him that he didn't know what she did in the afternoons. He usually had her back in her cabin by four, and didn't see her again 'til seven.

"I'm a napper. I go back to my room and nap for a couple of hours between morning stuff and evening. Trust me, you don't want to be around a sleep-deprived Bridget."

He grinned. "I'm sure it's not that bad."

Bridget's face was serious. "Oh, trust me. It's that bad. Ask Kaya if you have to. I'm a bear when I don't get enough sleep."

"I'll keep that in mind."

Her parents were gone again when he dropped her off at the cabin. "Where do they go every day?" he asked.

She shrugged. "I have no idea. I know Mom's helped Kaya with a few last-minute details with the reception, but I think mostly they've been exploring the ranch and the area. They love it here."

"And what about my Bridget? Does she love it here?"

Bridget nodded slowly. "I do. It snowed yesterday. I hate that it doesn't snow often in North Texas. And I love the mountains and the lake. This place has got to be what God meant when he made paradise."

"I agree. I fell in love with it when I came here for college, and I just couldn't leave. I think it's the most beautiful place on earth." He leaned down and brushed his lips across hers. "Sleep sweet, as my foster mom always used to say. I'll see you at seven."

Bridget nodded, hurrying into the cabin, and leaning back against the door. *How am I going to be able to leave him? Even if it is just for two weeks?*

* * *

That night when Kevin arrived, he stepped inside, looking around. "Are your parents out again?"

"Yup," Bridget said. "They're out dancing again. They go as often as they can. Mom says it's how she stays in shape."

"I ordered from the restaurant tonight. One of the waiters is going to bring our food into the library."

"Sounds good to me." She locked the door behind him. "You didn't bring your car?"

He shook his head. "I thought a nice brisk walk would be nice tonight." He'd already begun the modifications to his car for the reception, so he couldn't let her see it. Besides, walking in frigid air was good for them.

Bridget shrugged. She could deal with that. They went straight to the library as always, and she set up *Pocahontas* as the first movie. "She's not really a Disney princess, but she counts as one for our purposes."

Kevin didn't care what they did honestly. As long as he was able to spend more time with her. He'd started putting his plan in motion that afternoon, and he knew it was going to be interesting. "So you're booked all day tomorrow? Up until the reception?"

She nodded. "I could take a couple hours in the morning maybe. It would be tight, though."

"No need. I'll pick you up about seven. Will that work?" The reception started at seven, but she was allowed to be a little late according to her sister. He'd talked to her several times since the previous evening, setting his plan into motion.

"Yeah. I'm surprised Mom isn't insisting I be there early like she and Dad will be, but I'm not complaining. I'd rather go with you than with my family any day."

He grinned. "I like hearing that. You know I'm in love with you, don't you?"

She frowned. "I don't think you can fall in love that fast!"

"You honestly don't?"

She bit her lip. "Well, I didn't think so last week."

"And now?"

"I don't know. I mean I feel so much for you. So much

more than I'd ever expected to feel for anyone, but I've only known you a few days. It's probably just a vacation fling or something."

"Have you had a vacation fling before?"

She shook her head. "Not really. I've met some men while on vacation, but they didn't consume my every thought."

"I consume your every thought?" he asked with a grin. "I like this."

"I don't!" Bridget turned away from him and looked at the television which had just stopped playing the previews. "Movie's on."

Kevin watched her for the first minute or two of the movie, trying to figure out what was going on in her head, but maybe it was best if he didn't know.

The waiter, Steve, came in a few minutes later, setting down a small feast for each of them. Kevin passed off his credit card. "I'll bring the dishes to the kitchen myself later tonight."

"No need," the waiter told him. "I'll come and get them at the end of my shift. I'll have this back to you in just a minute."

Bridget looked down at the two plates, one held several slices of pizza and the other had a mountain of spaghetti and meat sauce. "Which is mine?"

He shrugged. "You take your pick. Or we can split both."

"I like the idea of having some of each if you don't mind."

"I don't mind at all."

While they watched the movie, they munched on the pizza and spaghetti, sharing bites off each other's plates. "You forgot your dessert in my car, so I brought it."

"Smart man."

By the time the first movie was over, they were finished, and the waiter had discreetly brought the credit card back. "They're great about accommodating here," she said as she switched movies. "I have been really impressed so far."

"It's an amazing place all around," Kevin told her. "I wish you'd been here in a warmer month for the swimming and white water rafting."

"I'm sure it would have been lots of fun. I want to do it, but I'm sure I'll come back sometime in the summer." She didn't want him to know that she'd applied for the nursing position until she made the final decision about whether or not she'd take it if it was offered. She loved her sister, and wanted to live closer to her, but if they spent a whole lot of time together, they'd kill each other. There was no doubt about that.

"I hope you'll be here in the summers sometimes. I can't let you go back to Texas on Monday without a promise of coming back."

Bridget sat back down beside him, her head automatically going to his shoulder. She didn't respond, because she didn't want to give too much away, but she couldn't imagine life without him. At all. How could she be alone after having him by her side?

Kevin took her silence as a good sign. She may not be talking about what she was thinking, but she wasn't arguing with him. That was good.

Walking back to the cabin that evening, he asked, "Why didn't you ask me if I'd made my decision yet?"

"You told me you refused to talk about it anymore today. So I didn't bring it up. Now if you want to voluntarily tell me what your decision is, I surely won't argue."

He shook his head, his arm around her shoulders. "I'm

not telling you anything. I'll just keep watching Disney like it's going out of style."

"Disney would never go out of style! Have you lost your mind? Disney is classic—and classics last forever and ever."

"You're not going to tell me we have to honeymoon at Disney, are you?"

"I haven't agreed to go on a honeymoon, so I can't answer that. You know you can't just keep hinting around that you plan to marry me and keep me around forever. One of these days you're going to have to actually ask me."

"I do know that." Kevin's words were soft, but they were heartfelt. He would ask as soon as he was ready, which might be sooner than she thought it would be.

"I'm going to miss you while you're getting all dolled up tomorrow. What color is your dress?"

"It's a pale blue, and it's more of a ball gown than anything else. Kaya said it would suit me. I feel silly in it, but if it makes her happy, I'll do it."

"I'm sure you'll be beautiful in it."

She shrugged. "Kaya's going to be impossible to be around tomorrow. I'll need to make sure I have my shrimp forks with me."

"You won't really stab her with one, will you?"

"Does a pregnant woman crave tacos? Of course I'm going to stab her!"

He stopped walking. "I don't know. Do pregnant women crave tacos?"

She nodded. "I poll all the pregnant patients I run into. Our practice is mostly family practice, but there are two OBs that are part of the practice, so I get to help with sonograms and stuff."

"You want kids, don't you?"

She laughed. "I want at least a dozen. Who doesn't want kids?"

He had no answer for her. He'd never even thought about having children. Of course, he'd do anything for his Bridget. Anything at all.

Chapter Eight

BRIDGET WOKE after ten the following morning, having slept late deliberately so she could stay up without her usual nap. Even when she was working, she napped as soon as she got home, so she wouldn't be grumpy. She just seemed to need more sleep than your average hibernating bear on sleeping pills.

She soaked in the hot tub on the back porch first thing, knowing she wouldn't want to mess up her hair later. She needed to be relaxed for the big day they had planned... and for all the time she was going to spend with her sister. There were no pockets in her dress for the reception, and she knew she needed to have her shrimp forks on her!

At noon, Kaya arrived and the three women walked over to the café together. "What do you think Kelsi is really going to name the baby?" Bridget asked. "She keeps calling her Herberta."

Kaya shrugged. "I don't think she'll name her Herberta, but my friend May is pregnant, and she is swearing up and down if the baby's a girl it will be Bobbette. Bob is insisting."

"Wait, didn't you tell me your friend May had a crush on that guy Bob Bodefeld from the show *Lazy Love*? She married a guy named Bob?" Bridget almost made an off-color comment, but she remembered her mother was there. The sad thing was Mom didn't mind off-color comments. She used them as a spring board to embarrass her daughters. Nope. Not happening. When Bridget and Kaya had been young, they'd both refused to listen to the sex-talk, so their mother had taken them for a drive. Going down the highway at seventy-five miles per hour was the best time to talk about sex according to Vicki Taylor!

"Yup. May actually married Bob Bodefeld. She met him on a plane shortly after leaving the ranch. They were married less than a week later. And she got pregnant right away."

"Bobbette is a terrible name. Does May now how bad the name is?"

Kaya shrugged. "With as many books as May has written, she says she needs a break from naming people, so she doesn't care what Bob names the baby. I think it will be either Robert Junior, and they'll call him Bobby, or Bobbette, and they'll call her Bobbi. She worries me."

"I hope you don't give Glen carte blanche with naming your first child," Mom told Kaya. "I don't think he'd come up with a horrible name like that, but you just can't trust men to name children. Dad kept begging me to name you two Lucretia and Leia."

"So he could call us Luke and Leia? The man is an evil genius!" Kaya laughed out loud. "Just so I got to be Leia and Bridget got stuck with Lucretia."

Bridget made a face and brandished her shrimp fork. "Be nice. I have a weapon, and I'm not afraid to use it."

Kaya pulled out her own shrimp fork. "I'm not afraid of you, Cinderella freak!"

"Better than being a Belle freak."

Kevin stopped walking and stared at the twins. "Bridget?"

"I told you I stabbed her with shrimp forks," Bridget said, blushing as she stuck the fork behind her back. She felt like a small child who had been caught with her hand in the cookie jar.

Kevin shook his head. "I should have known you weren't joking. Where are you ladies headed?"

"To the café for lunch," Kaya responded, sticking her tongue out at her sister. "Want to join us?"

"I would, but I've got plans. I'm going to pick up my boxed lunch that Kelsi made me and keep working."

Bridget frowned. "What are you working on today anyway? You never told me."

He shrugged, hurrying ahead to open the door for them. "It's good to see you, Mrs. Taylor."

"Are you hiding something from me?" Bridget asked, surprised he wouldn't tell her what he was doing. It wasn't like him from what she could tell. Of course she'd only known him for a few days.

"It's a surprise for you, so not hiding something bad from you, just needing it to be a surprise." He didn't meet her gaze as he said it, and her mind immediately taunted her.

"Okay." She walked past him toward the table with Mom and Kaya, refusing to spare another glance.

He caught her arm. "Don't be mad, Bridget."

"I'm not mad. I'm fine." She wasn't though. She wasn't fine at all. "I'll see you tonight." Unless he stood her up or something.

He watched her get into the booth with her mom and sister for a moment, before finally turning away. He didn't have a lot of time to placate her, and she'd understand soon enough.

Walking to the counter, he got the boxed lunch he'd ordered and paid for it.

Bridget refused to watch Kevin leave, but she knew where he was the entire time he was there. And she knew when he left. Her entire heart sank. She tried to pay attention to her sister and mother, but she just didn't care what they were saying.

A hand was in front of her face. "Bridget, will you wake up and pay attention?" Kaya asked, obviously frustrated.

"Sorry. What did you say?"

"We were talking about the order of the dances tonight. The first will be me with Glen, the second me with dad while Glen dances with his mom, and the third will be Glen's dad with me, while Mom dances with Glen."

Bridget blinked a couple of times. "Oh, I didn't know you were dancing with Glen's dad."

"Yup. And you haven't met Dawna yet, but she's Glen's kid sister. You two are going to have to become friends. It's a *moral necessity!*"

Bridget nodded absently. Kaya was always claiming different things were a moral necessity. Bridget frequently thought that Kaya should have been an actress, because she was so dramatic about everything. Kaya said she'd settle for creating emotions on paper instead of through theater or movies. "Sure. I'll be her friend."

Kaya stabbed Bridget in the arm with her shrimp fork. "What's your problem? This is the day I've been planning for months, and you are *not* going to be a wet blanket!"

Bridget shook her head, refusing to let Kevin get to her. No, she wouldn't be a wet blanket. "No problem at all. What else do I need to know about the reception?"

Kaya went on and on about the special plans she'd made, and Mom nodded with each thing.

After they'd ordered, Mom pulled a bag she'd brought with her off the booth beside her and gave each of the sisters a book. Bridget flipped through hers and burst out laughing. "You scrapbooked every single photo we took on our cruise?"

When she and Kaya had gone on a cruise to be bridesmaids for their best friend, Jenni, they had gotten a little… crazy. They were left to their own devices entirely too much, so they had run around the ship after dinner every night taking pictures with each of the photographers. There were six. And they took several pictures with each. Every. Single. Night. There were more than two hundred photos by the time they were done, and they'd each purchased an unlimited photo package, which meant there were more photos than either of them knew what to do with or cared to have. And then there were the selfies they'd taken with the photographers, because they'd wanted to remember them.

By the last night all of the photographers had greeted them by name and had them do very silly things. There were a couple pictures where they were standing back to back, both of them looking angry. Bridget knew those photos were her favorites. She looked up from the book. "I love both of you so much. Even you, Kaya."

Kaya laughed. Her photo album was identical, except hers had Belle on the front, while Bridget's had Cindy. "Thanks, Mom. These are perfect. I just wish we had one for Jenni."

Bridget shook her head. "Jenni does not want to remember us doing that on her wedding cruise!"

"Probably not. She had no sense of humor about it." Kaya shook her head. "She was convinced her new husband would think less of her for our shrimp fork shenanigans."

"Did you ever write that book?"

"Not yet. I'm working up to it. I think Shrimp Fork Shenanigans needs to be my absolute best work. So I'm working on it little by little."

"You could also call it Teasing in Texas, you know."

Kaya cocked her head to one side, before nodding. "I think you should be my new title creator. You're good at it!"

"Pay me what I'm making now, and I'm all over it."

"Umm…don't quit your day job!"

Mom shook her head at the two of them as their food was put on the table in front of them. Joni was serving again, which Bridget hated. "Where's Kelsi? She was at her obstetrician's appointment yesterday. Where is she today?" Bridget tried to keep the whine out of her voice, but she missed her friend.

"She doesn't work on Saturdays. I think she'll be cutting down on her hours soon anyway. She's getting just a little too round to work that much." Joni smiled. "Sorry you had to put up with me two days in a row."

"It's not that. It just doesn't feel right to be here without her!"

Joni nodded emphatically. "It doesn't feel right to me either. And I've worked here for a long while. Kelsi belongs at Kelsey's Kafé! Let me know if you need anything!"

Mom grabbed one of the fried cheese curds and bit into it. "Wait…why is this the first time I've been here? And we're leaving Monday. I will be here for lunch tomorrow!"

Kaya bit her lip. "Umm…Mom? They're closed on Sundays. You can come for breakfast on Monday before your flight!"

"Closed on Sundays? What is this? No, I refuse to believe they're closed tomorrow. I'll be here."

Kaya shook her head and said, "Okay." Kaya and Bridget exchanged a look. One thing that had always united them was their mother's special brand of insanity.

Bridget changed the subject. "I've been indoctrinating Kevin all week."

"Pastor Kevin? Isn't he already indoctrinated enough? He's a pastor after all."

"Not on the ways of Disney!"

Kaya rolled her eyes. "You know as well as I do that Belle is the best. I don't know why you persist in dragging others into this. She's the only princess who reads!"

"In the live-action Cinderella, she reads."

"Yeah. She does. What took her so long to get there?" Kaya crossed her eyes at her sister.

"Mom, Kaya's being a brat."

"You know, I was ecstatic when I found out I would be having twins. I was so excited to have two children, when doctors never thought I'd have any, and then when I found out I was having two girls, I thought, 'How wonderful! They'll have built-in best friends for life.' Reality really slapped me in the face with you two."

Bridget sighed. "I love Kaya. She's just annoying."

"And I love Bridget. We'll get along. I promise." Kaya took her shrimp fork and jabbed Bridget in the thigh under the table where their mother couldn't see.

Bridget grinned and returned the favor, and the two of them continuously stabbed each other for the rest of the meal. When the check was brought, their mother pounced on it, and Bridget sighed. "I can pay for a meal every once in a while." She hadn't even been allowed to pay for her share of the cabin. And she'd wanted to! She finally had a well-paying job, and she hated that she couldn't use her money to help her mother out from time to time.

"I know. My turn."

Bridget rolled her eyes. "It's always your turn." She looked at Kaya. "Where's the spa we're going to?"

"Oh, we're doing the ranch spa. It's between here and the main house. Sheila, who has done Kelsi's hair her whole life is going to do an up-do for you this afternoon. I think you should go with a Cinderella bun. Do you have a tiara?"

Bridget wrinkled her nose. "You're the one who got married. You should have a tiara. You're not wearing a white dress to this thing, are you?"

"I'm not. I'm wearing an off-white tea length though."

"How come you get tea length and I get the huge ball gown look? Not fair!"

"You'll be the belle of the ball!"

"You know I'd rather be Cinderella."

Kaya rolled her eyes. "If you don't want to do a tiara, I have a headband in that shade of blue. Want to try that?"

"I guess. What's up with you and my hair? Shouldn't you be worried about your hair?"

"Why? My hair is fine the way it is. Besides, I don't have the length to fuss with like you do." Kaya's hair was not quite shoulder length, while Bridget's was halfway down her back. "I just think you should let Sheila try."

"Okay. It's your reception."

"It is! It's my party, and I'll fix your hair like I want to!" Kaya sang the words to the tune of "It's my party." Well, she tried to sing to that tune. Her singing was just as bad as Bridget's.

"Sure. I'll do what you want." Bridget frowned. It wasn't like she'd be here much longer. No one would remember what she looked like in a month. She needed to tell Wade to pull her application. She wouldn't be able to stand seeing Kevin every day and knowing he was keeping secrets from her.

When they got to the spa, Bridget was taken to a massage room by a girl named Maddie who talked to her for a moment. "Do you have any problem areas I need to address?"

Bridget shook her head. "Nope, and I've never had a massage so just do your thing, and even if you mess up, I won't know the difference."

"I'm not going to mess up." Maddie shook her head. "I'm really good at what I do. I promise."

"Okay."

"You need to get undressed and under the sheet. You can leave your panties on if you're more comfortable that way. I'll be back in about five minutes, and then we'll begin."

Bridget stripped fast. She didn't even know how long it took to take her clothes off. What if it took her five and a half minutes, and Maddie walked in and saw her naked? As a nurse, she was used to seeing others naked, but she didn't want people seeing *her* naked!

She was lying on the table with her eyes closed when the door opened a tiny bit. "Are you ready?"

"Yes, come in!"

"Let me know if my pressure is too strong or too little. You need to enjoy it." Maddie started with her shoulders and began rubbing. Bridget enjoyed it so much, she just closed her eyes and drifted away.

The next thing she knew, Maddie was having her roll over. "I must have fallen asleep!" Bridget yawned.

Maddie laughed. "Then I'm doing my job right."

When it was over, Bridget thanked Maddie for the massage and got dressed, wandering out to the main desk and sitting down beside Kaya. "How was your massage?" Kaya asked.

"I don't know. I slept the whole time! I feel a lot less tense, though."

"Good. I wonder how Mom is liking hers."

"She probably loves it. She gets massages sometimes, I think. Doesn't she? I'm pretty sure she does. I'm not even sure." Bridget shrugged. "I haven't lived with Mom for a few years, so I'm not up on what she does every day. I think I talk to her more than you do, though."

"My hours are so weird, it's hard to talk to real people." Kaya shrugged. "Oh well, I like my life as it is."

"How does it work for you and Glen with you up all night and him working all day?"

"It's not a big deal. He goes to work about eight, and I've usually been in bed for an hour or two. I get up an hour before he gets off work, and I play the wife game and cook dinner. I do some housework while it cooks, and we spend our evenings together. He goes to bed around eleven, and that's when I start working. It works well."

"I guess so. Just still seems weird." Bridget refused to think about how she and Kevin would be able to mesh their schedules easier, because she wasn't going to be with Kevin. How had he become so entwined in her life in such a short time? Six days. This was the sixth day she'd known him, and her mind was already a mess. *This* was why she didn't get involved with men!

"Works for us. I know it's weird, but I like not sharing a bed. I mean, we sleep in the same bed, but at different times. No one is fighting over the covers and no one keeps someone else awake with their snoring. Very peaceful."

Mom walked into the room then. "What's next?"

"Hair. We're all three getting washes and styles, and Bridget's getting an up-do."

Bridget started to protest, but decided not to waste her time. Kaya pulled a blue ribbon from her purse and handed it to the woman working on Bridget's hair, and she pulled out a picture of Cinderella. "Just like that."

Bridget stared at her sister and shook her head. "You've lost your mind."

Kaya just shrugged and ignored Bridget for the rest of their hair time.

They all sat together while they got their toes done, talking and laughing. Mom rubbed the back of her neck. "I just wish my chiropractor had come with me. I need to be adjusted badly."

The girl sitting on a little stool at Bridget's feet looked up at that. "We have one here in the spa. Do you want to see her?"

"There's one working here today?"

"Yes. She works Tuesday through Saturday."

"Really? Yes, I want to see her. I threw my hip out dancing last night, and someone has got to put it back in."

The girl stood. "I'll go get her and you can talk while we finish up."

A tall, slender brunette came into the room. "I'm Dr. Michelle. Who needs an adjustment?" She had a look of concern on her face as she walked over to Mom and poked her shoulder.

"It's not my shoulder that hurts," Mom told her. "It's my hip. I threw it out dancing last night, and I need it shoved back in so I can go to my daughter's wedding reception tonight, and dance until my feet hurt too much to stand."

Dr. Michelle nodded. "When your toes are dry, have them bring you to see me. I'll take good care of you."

Glen came in while they sat in the waiting room waiting for Mom. "You ladies look beautiful." He took

Kaya's hand and drew her to him, kissing her. "You especially."

Kaya smiled. "Sometimes I think you have vision issues, but I'm very glad you do."

"You ready?"

"Yeah." Kaya turned to Bridget. "I'm going to go home and get ready. Remind Mom to be there at six thirty."

Bridget nodded. "I will."

While she sat waiting for her mother, Bridget's mind tormented her. What was going on with Kevin? Why was he hiding something? Did he have a girlfriend there on the ranch already? If he did, why was he going around openly with her? It didn't make sense, but she couldn't think of anything else he'd hide from her.

When her mom came out, they walked back to the cabin in silence. "I'm going to go read for a bit. Kaya said to remind you to be there at six thirty."

Mom nodded, giving Bridget a quick hug. "Trust him."

Bridget frowned as she walked away. What did her mother know that she didn't?

Chapter Nine

THE DRESS KAYA had picked out for Bridget to wear was a floor length light blue gown, made out of a silky material, but when Bridget went to the closet to get the dress, she realized it wasn't the one her sister had chosen. It was the same color as the previous one, but it had a much fuller skirt.

She pulled it out and laid it on the bed. "Mom! This isn't the dress I'm supposed to wear! What happened to my dress?"

Mom hurried into Bridget's bedroom and looked at the dress, her face a mask of innocence. "I have no idea. You'll have to wear that one."

"Mom, this looks like a Cinderella costume. I cannot wear a Cinderella costume to my sister's wedding reception."

"Well, the dress is formal enough for the reception. This thing is going to be formal. You'll have to just wear what you have."

Bridget frowned. "I don't know. I'm going to feel very

out of place. This is something for a formal ball—or Halloween!"

"You're just going to have to suck it up. I don't know what else to tell you. It's time for us to leave." Mom was already dressed in a mid-calf length emerald green dress that was pure elegance.

"I don't know. I'd feel better in jeans than in this fancy thing. What happened to the dress I was supposed to wear?"

Dad stuck his head into the room. "It's time to go, Vicki."

"Dad, do you know anything about my dress? This isn't the one I agreed to wear."

"I don't know nothing about no dress. I've never worn one myself." He shrugged. "Looks pretty. You should wear it."

Bridget groaned. She wasn't going to get any answers from them. When her dad put on his country boy act and started using double negatives, she knew he was being evasive, but what could she do?

She sighed, and watched her parents disappear. Kevin was supposed to be there in ten minutes, and she needed to be dressed when he got there. There was nothing to do but put on the silly ball gown.

She slipped into it, frowning down at the full skirt. She felt like she'd stepped straight out of *Gone With the Wind*, but there really wasn't anything else for her to wear. She stepped into the bathroom and quickly added a touch of make-up, and then she looked for her shoes. She was supposed to have heels to wear. Where were her heels? In their place were ballet slippers. How on earth was she supposed to make those work? It had snowed again while she was soaking in the hot tub.

Bridget wanted nothing more than to admit defeat and

stay in the cabin crying all night. Kevin was up to something, and she had no idea what. The dress was all wrong. She was going to look like a fool.

She took a deep breath and looked at herself in the mirror. The dress was beautiful, and she did feel a bit like a princess wearing it. She would never see these people again. In fact, while Kevin was dancing with Jaclyn, which she would encourage with everything inside her, she'd go talk to Wade and let him know that she was rescinding her job application. She was not going to work and live on this ranch. There was no way she could!

The knock at the door came at exactly seven, and she hurried and opened it, her gaze landing on Kevin's broad shoulders in a formal suit. She'd never seen him in anything but jeans, and she felt the breath knocked out of her. He was something else.

His tie matched her dress perfectly, and he had a fancy handkerchief that matched tucked into his suit pocket. "You look absolutely amazing," he said, slightly out of breath himself.

Bridget gave him a half smile. Why was he even trying? She was leaving in thirty-six hours, and he had someone else he was interested in anyway. Maybe there was a new guest on the ranch who he'd spent the day with. That had to be it.

He offered her one arm, and she took it, turning to lock the door. When they got to his car, she stopped short. There was a huge pumpkin taped to the top of his car with what looked like orange duct tape. "Umm…Kevin?"

"Yes?"

"You do realize you have a pumpkin taped to the top of your car, don't you?"

"Yes, I do."

Bridget nodded. "All right. I was just making sure you knew about it." *He's lost his mind. I need to proceed cautiously.*

He opened the passenger door for her. "Your coach awaits you, milady."

"Milady?" Bridget couldn't help but giggle. Men with Texas accents could *not* say milady without making people laugh. *What is he up to?*

He hurried around and got behind the wheel, driving them the short distance to the main ranch house. "They're working on a bigger venue for parties like this that will be in a barn. Well, it'll be built to look like a barn, but no actual animals will have pooped in it."

This was the Kevin she knew and loved. The one talking about cow poop while they were all dressed up and looking fancy. "I'm sure this one will be big enough for *this* party."

"I'm sure it will."

He stopped behind the main house, and hurried around to get her door for her. He'd never displayed that type of old-fashioned manners before, and she wondered again what was going on with him.

He tucked her hand behind his elbow and hurried to the door, opening it wide. "You ready?"

She nodded. "I guess so. I feel like I'm a bit over-dressed, but the dress I was supposed to wear disappeared!"

When they walked in, she spotted Kaya with Glen over on the other side of the room, and she immediately started walking in that direction with Kevin keeping pace with her. "Where's the dress I was supposed to wear?" she hissed in her sister's ear. "I feel like a fool."

"You look gorgeous," Kaya whispered. "Just go with it!"

"Go with what? Kevin's acting weird, there was this

strange pumpkin on top of his car held there by duct tape, and my dress was missing! *What's going on?*"

"You'll understand in a little while." Kaya turned back to the woman in front of her, greeting her calmly. "Lily, this is my twin sister Bridget. Bridget, this is Lily Donahue. She's the event coordinator here at the ranch. I never could have pulled this off without her."

Bridget smiled at the woman. "It's nice to meet you."

Lily nodded. "You too." She turned back to Kaya, asking about how she liked the decorations.

Bridget sighed, standing beside her sister until it was time to eat. She was seated at the main table with Kevin, Glen and his parents, Dawna, Kaya, and her parents.

When they had been served their chicken dinners by the wait staff, Kevin said a prayer for the entire room, and sat down beside her. His hand squeezed hers under the table.

As soon as the meal was over, the dancing began. After the first obligatory dances of the newlyweds with each other and parents, Kevin bowed low over Bridget's hand. "May I have this dance?"

Bridget frowned. "You're really starting to creep me out, Kevin."

He just grinned at her, leading her to the dance floor even though there was no music playing. At his nod to the small band that was playing, the song "Stealing Cinderella" filled the room. Bridget had only heard the song a few times, and it had always made her cry.

She looked up at him with a question in her eyes that she wasn't sure how to voice. No one joined them on the dance floor as they slowly spun around. She leaned forward and rested her forehead against his shoulder. If he had another woman in his life, he certainly wasn't acting like it tonight. Tonight, he acted as if she was the only woman in the room—no, the only woman in the whole world!

As the music finally died down, he brushed his lips across her forehead. "Tonight, you're my Cinderella."

Her eyes widened as she finally understood. "Is that why there was a pumpkin duct taped to the top of your car?"

"Yes. I thought you'd get it right away."

He led her to a chair back at the table where they'd been sitting. "You sure you don't need a fairy godmother to help you out tonight, Kevin?" a voice asked out of nowhere. Bridget turned and saw that it was Jaclyn, dressed in a pretty pink dress. When she looked closely, she could see fairies embroidered on the collar. They were tiny, but they were there.

Kevin made a face. "I'm sure."

"You look like you might need some help." Jaclyn stood behind him, her hands on her hips, looking quite persistent.

"No, I've got it. Thank you so much for the offer though." Kevin turned back to Bridget. "Is there anything I can get you? There's a nice selection of desserts to choose from over along a table."

Bridget grinned. "Dessert? You're treating me like Cinderella and bringing me desserts? What have I done in my life to deserve to spend a glorious week with a man like you?"

Kevin frowned slightly, but his plan wasn't completed yet. He was going to make this work. "What do you want?"

"You know what I like. We've been sharing desserts all week. Find me something yummy."

Jaclyn took Kevin's chair as he walked off. "He's trying really hard to make you happy, Bridget. His methods may seem a little strange, but he loves you."

Bridget frowned. "Are you sure? He refused to tell me what he was doing all day."

"Someone had to duct tape that pumpkin to his car, didn't they?" Jaclyn rose and patted Bridget's shoulder. "Let him treat you like his princess for the evening."

Bridget watched her walk away, a bit startled when two desserts landed on the table in front of her. "The restaurant here specializes in huckleberry pie, so I got you a piece of that with extra whipped cream, and I thought you might like a piece of cheesecake. I haven't seen you try any cheesecake all week."

"Good choices." She reached into her cleavage and pulled out two shrimp forks. "I saw that you forgot the forks."

He blinked a few times. "I'm not sure I can eat off of this."

"A little boob sweat never hurt anyone." She cut into the pie and ate a bite, closing her eyes with pleasure. "That's yummy."

Kevin stared at the fork in his hand, trying to figure out the right thing to do. Eating off a fork that had been in her cleavage was stranger than he was ready to get at the moment.

A fork appeared before his face, and he turned and smiled at Kaya. "Thank you."

"Merry Christmas," she whispered as she hurried away.

Kelsi walked by then, her dress showing off her baby bump and making it look bigger than it had all week. "How was the doctor's appointment?" Bridget asked.

"It's good. Baby's growing like she should. We're going to have a healthy little Shania soon."

"Shania?"

Kelsi nodded happily. "Her daddy's name is Shane after all."

Bridget shrugged. "Better than Herberta, I guess."

"What isn't?" Shane asked, smiling.

A moment later, another couple came to the table, and Bridget recognized the woman as Belinda, the girl who had been in the café with Kelsi, bumping bellies against her will. "Hi, Bridget. Are you having fun?"

Bridget nodded. "I am. I feel a little silly in this dress, but I'm having fun."

"I think your dress is perfect," Kelsi said. "For a Cinderella lover anyway."

Bridget sighed, looking down at the full skirt. "I just want to know where the dress I was supposed to wear went. And why I ended up with this one!"

Kelsi shrugged. "Don't complain. Go with it!" The band started playing an upbeat song, and Kelsi squealed. "Ask me to dance, Shane Clapper!"

Shane grinned at his boisterous wife. "Would you care to dance, Kelsi?"

"Let me think…yes!" She grabbed his hand and pulled him to the dance floor.

Belinda smiled as she watched them. "Aren't you guys going to dance?" she asked Bridget.

"Can't at the moment. I have two desserts to share with Kevin."

"I can see that's a lot more important than dancing!" Belinda laughed and wandered away, pulling her husband behind her.

"Who is her husband? What's his name? He didn't say a single word!" Bridget looked to Kevin for her answer. She looked to him for answers to a lot of things, she'd found.

"That's Wyatt Weston. He's in charge of the stables, and Glen's boss."

"Okay!" Bridget went back to savoring her dessert, surprised at the steady stream of people who stopped by to meet her.

She was thankfully good with names or she'd never have remembered them all. She met Elf, the man who had just been hired to be the blacksmith on property, and he was also in charge of general maintenance. He said he was Ellie and Dink's brother.

Then Ellie, the wife of the riverman there on the ranch, came by with her husband Will to chat for a minute. "Those desserts look good, but I'm holding out for wedding cake," Will said. "Oh, who am I kidding? I'm going to have some of everything. Come on, Ellie!"

Kevin smiled and whispered, "Those two were the first people I married on the ranch. Love them."

"They seem nice."

Jess and Jake came over and introduced themselves as local veterinarians. Jess's eyes struck Bridget. "You must be related to the Westons. Your eyes are a dead giveaway." Every Weston she'd met so far had ice blue eyes.

Jess nodded. "I'm their cousin. I was raised here on the ranch with them."

"It's very nice to meet you. I guess you work with Glen some."

Jake shrugged. "A little. I think we'll be working more closely with him when he has his equestrian ranch up and running."

Wes Weston and his new wife, Amber, wandered by. "I heard you did a little bit of Bigfoot hunting. Did you find anything?"

Bridget shook her head. "No, but I wanted to. Why does everyone laugh when they say that? If I were a Bigfoot, I'd choose to live in this area for sure."

Kelsi dragged another woman over by the hand.

Bridget looked back and forth between the two of them, realizing this must be Dani. She'd been wanting to meet her. "Wow…you two really do emphasize the differences, don't you?"

Dani shrugged. She was wearing a pair of nice slacks and a pretty blouse, instead of the formal gown her sister wore. "We were dressed alike until we were old enough to refuse to go to school that way ever again."

Bridget laughed. "Kaya and I were dressed alike when we were little as well, but there isn't another set of twins who looks more different."

"Oh, I don't know," Dani said, obviously thinking about it. "I can see it in your facial features, but your coloring and size are so different. I mean, you're both slender, but Kaya has to be over six foot."

"And I'm much shorter," Bridget said with a shrug. "She calls me Bridget the Midget, which isn't exactly flattering."

"It's definitely a sister thing." Dani looked at her desserts. "Oh, there's pie? Where?"

Bridget pointed in the direction of the dessert tables, and as the sisters walked away, she turned to Kevin. "They couldn't be more different."

Kevin shook his head. "No, they couldn't. You and Kaya are more alike than they are."

"I wonder if they ever stab each other with shrimp forks." She'd always been curious about other sets of twins, wanting to get inside their heads.

"I can't believe you brought shrimp forks to your sister's wedding reception *in your cleavage!* What is wrong with you?"

"Do you want a written list, or can you just take mental notes?"

He laughed, shaking his head. "You know, you are a *very* unique woman. I think that's why I love you so much."

Bridget frowned. "What did you do all day?"

He sighed. "I got ready for tonight in my own way."

"Like taping a pumpkin to the top of your car?"

"Yes, and a few other things you haven't seen yet." He shrugged. "And I had to go find a tie and a handkerchief that matched your dress. That was important."

"You're a good man, Kevin Roberts."

A man Bridget didn't recognize walked over then. "We're going to miss your attitude at the café when you go."

"My attitude?" Bridget asked. She knew that voice. She'd heard it yelling just yesterday. "Bob! You've been cooking for me all week!"

"I have. And you've been appreciative, which is nice. Did Joni really say I had a big head?"

Bridget laughed. "She did. Is that a problem?"

"I'm not sure yet. I may have to say something to her about it. Or maybe I'll put a bobblehead with my picture over the face on the counter in the kitchen at work. That's what I'll do. And if she says something, I'll tell her it's her fault, because she said I have a big head!"

"I think that's a brilliant idea. Who doesn't want a Bob bobblehead around?"

Bob nodded and hurried off.

Bridget smiled. "I love this place. The people here are really amazing. You can feel the love between them, and I don't mean just the newly married couples, of which there seem to be a *lot*."

"Come dance with me."

Bridget nodded. "Sounds good." She followed him out to the dance floor and couldn't help but laugh when the opening strains to "Beauty and the Beast" started playing. "You arranged these songs in advance, didn't you?"

"I'll never tell!"

As soon as the dance was over, he caught her hand, and pulled her to a chair that was in the middle of the dance floor. She hadn't seen it there before, and she couldn't help but wonder where it had come from. It seemed to have appeared by magic as soon as the song finished playing. She looked around for Jaclyn, knowing that magic on the ranch had to have come from her, but Jaclyn was busy talking to an older man, and not paying her any attention.

She sat down, because it seemed to be what Kevin wanted from her, and she frowned up at him. What was he up to? She almost felt like she'd been living in her favorite fairytale tonight, but why? *Is he giving me a send-off I'll never forget? Or was he asking me to stay?*

Kevin nodded at someone she couldn't see, and Bob appeared at his side, holding a silk pillow in the same shade of blue as her dress. On top of it was a red cowboy boot, balanced precariously. She wanted to laugh at how silly the boot looked on a pillow, but he was obviously trying to make a very grand gesture, and she wasn't about to ruin it for him. Or anyone else. Bob seemed to care very much about whatever it was they were doing there.

Bridget stared at the boot in confusion as Kevin plucked it from the pillow and knelt on the floor at her feet. "Cinderella should always be given a shoe by her prince, but we're on a ranch, so I thought a cowboy boot would be more acceptable."

Bridget laughed. "Does this mean you're my prince?" Could a pastor even *be* a prince? Was that legal?

"It means I want to be." Kevin removed the ballet

slipper from her foot and carefully pushed the cowboy boot on. "Will you be my Cinderella?"

"Of course, I'm your Cinderella. Does this mean you've made your choice?" Had he done all this to tell her that Cinderella was his favorite princess?

He sighed. "I'm a Cinderella man. How could I choose another princess, when *my* princess's opinion is really the only one that matters to me?"

She smiled, swiping away a tear. It was then she realized everyone in the whole room had gathered around them, including her family. Kevin turned to her father who had materialized beside her. "I'm going to do what the song said, Mr. Taylor. I'm stealing Cinderella."

"You can have her!"

Bridget frowned at her father. "Dad! That's not how the song goes! Weren't you listening to the words?"

Dad shrugged. "Who cares? If someone will take your mother, I'll give her away too!"

Everyone laughed at that, especially when he put his arm around Mom's shoulders and kissed her cheek. It was obvious he wasn't getting rid of his wife for anything.

Kevin turned back to Bridget. "I want you to be my Cinderella."

Bridget frowned. "I already said I would. I even let you put the boot on my foot!"

"I don't think you understand." He reached into the pocket of his suit and pulled out a box, opening it for her to see. "I want you to be my Cinderella for the rest of my life. Not just tonight."

Bridget stared at him in astonishment. When had he gotten an engagement ring? He'd gone to a lot of trouble to make sure everything was perfect so he could do this tonight. "I—"

"Please?"

Chapter Ten

Bridget felt her heart in her throat, well aware of all the people staring at her, waiting for her to agree to marry the man on one knee before her—the man she loved. "What about my job?" It was the only thing she could think to say to stall him, and he had to be stalled. At least for a little while.

"Your background checked out. The nursing job here on the ranch is yours—if you'll take it." Wade's voice was loud and strong. Bridget hadn't even realized he was there until that very moment.

Kevin looked at her expectantly. "See? It's settled. You have a job here."

Bridget felt her heart pound faster and faster, incredibly nervous to be the center of attention at such an important time. Finally, she let out a whoosh of air. "Can we talk privately? Please?"

Kevin's face fell as he nodded and got to his feet. If she wanted to talk privately, that could only mean one thing. She was going to refuse. He offered her his hand, and they walked together out of the circle of people surrounding them, and through the doors to the main part of the house. He led her to the library, where they'd spent so many evenings together.

Once they were both sitting on the couch, Bridget turned to him fully. "I wasn't expecting this. I thought you were with some other girl today, so you asking me to marry you this evening came as a real shock. I'm not sure what to say."

Kevin studied her face. "Start by telling me how you feel about me. I'm in love with you, Bridget, and I want to know there's a chance of a future between us."

"Kevin, I'm sure you know I love you. That's not my hesitation at all. I'm worried that I'll be a terrible pastor's wife. I know that you don't really have a congregation, but still, I feel like I need to act all proper and circumspect to be married to a pastor. I keep shrimp forks in my cleavage, for Bob's sake!"

Kevin blinked a few times. "For Bob's sake?"

She shrugged. "A friend of mine says that a lot, and I kind of like it. Don't you?"

"I have no idea how to even respond to that." He loved her quirkiness, but sometimes she said something so utterly unexpected that he had no clue how he should even begin to continue a discussion that had once been perfectly normal.

"Me neither. Anyway, I'm madly in love with you. I've known it for days. I haven't wanted to admit it, of course, because who falls in love in less than a week, but it's true." She sighed. "I just need a little time to answer you. I'm going to take the job here on the ranch, and I promise you'll have your answer within a month or so. Will that work?"

"A month? Are you kidding? That's forever."

She sighed. "Before I come back to the ranch? I just—I

see myself being in charge of teaching a women's Bible study and talking about entirely inappropriate things. I see myself planning a church pot luck and demanding everyone bring dessert, because who wants a real meal anyway? What if someone comes over one evening and I haven't had my nap, and I snap their head off?" Why couldn't he see that the struggle was real?

He sighed. "I guess I can wait for an answer. I'll be worse than a small child waiting for Santa Claus to come, but I'll do my best."

She leaned toward him and pressed her lips to his. "Have you ever kissed a princess before?"

"Can't say that I have, but I'm sure I like it!" He traced her cheek with one finger. "We need to get back to the reception." He looked down at the ring box still in his hand and snapped it shut. "I guess I'll keep this until you can figure out how to answer me."

"It's a beautiful ring." It had a large diamond surrounded by sapphires. She'd wear it with pride if she could make sure she wouldn't tarnish his reputation by doing it.

He put the ring back into his pocket and stood, offering her his hand. He noticed her toes peeking out from under her dress and had to laugh. "I guess I should either give you the other cowboy boot, or we should put your slipper back on you. I didn't notice you walking lopsided on the way here, but I'm sure you must have."

"Were you in cahoots with Kaya about how I should look tonight? My dress disappeared, and she insisted on a Cinderella hairdo."

"Of course, I was in cahoots with her. And your parents. Glen took the Cinderella dress to the cabin today while you were out getting pampered with your mom and sister. Your dad helped him swipe the one you were going to wear." He smiled. "Have I mentioned yet how very beautiful you look tonight? I want to keep you forever and ever."

"If we were the only two people in the world, or you had any other profession, the answer would be a no-brainer. I would marry you in a heartbeat."

"Even if I was an international assassin?"

Bridget blinked at him a couple of times. "An international assassin? Where did *that* come from?"

He shrugged. "One of the things I love best about you, my dear Bridget, is that you bring out my silly side. I tend to take myself too seriously, but you with your Cinderella obsession and shrimp forks in your cleavage make me realize that we're meant to laugh and have a good time in life. It's not all about being serious."

She smiled. "I taught you something. Wow. I wouldn't have thought that possible. I do like to enjoy life though. Sometimes you just need to go to Burger King and wear the silly hat."

"What?"

"Once when Kaya and I were teenagers, we went to Burger King, and they had those silly paper crowns. We wore them all day. Even to the mall. People were pointing at us and making fun of us, but we were laughing at ourselves too. It was a really fun day that I'll never forget."

"You have the ability to find joy in the tiniest of things. I think that's what I love most about you."

Bridget sighed, stepping toward him and wrapping her arms around him for a moment. "Thank you."

"For what?" He was sincerely baffled.

"For treating me like I'm perfectly normal to behave as I do. I know it's a little out of the realm of what people expect, but I can't let life be too serious. It doesn't work for me, and it makes me sad."

He took her hand and brought it to his lips. "Marry me, and I promise we'll find the humor in the world together."

She smiled. "I want to so badly. Just give me a few days."

He nodded, trying not to let his hurt show. He'd been certain if he'd done the big proposal, and made it Cinderella themed, she would agree on the spot. "Take the time you need."

She took his hand and led him back to the party. If anyone noticed she didn't have a shiny new engagement ring on her finger, they didn't say anything.

Bridget sat in the front row of the small church in the Old West town the following morning. She was more a back row and escape early before she could offend someone type girl, but for Kevin, she was willing to do just about anything. She went to church every Sunday, and had since she was a child, but she'd never felt so much a part of a sermon.

She was amazed at how casual he was in his preaching. He wore a pair of jeans and cowboy boots, and his shirt was a green checked button-up Western shirt. His message was simple. It was all about love, and went into detail about the three words in the New Testament that were translated into love in the English language.

There was no modern Christian band playing, and the people there simply sang hymns. She liked the feel of the church. It wasn't one of the modern mega-churches like she'd been a member of all her life. Instead it was simple and old-fashioned. Most of the people she'd met on the ranch were there that day, and they were all dressed in the same manner as Kevin.

Midway through his sermon on love, she had her answer. He was so calm and casual in his preaching, that she knew it wouldn't be a tough job to be his wife. She could do it. More than that, she couldn't *not* do it. A life without him in it wasn't something she even wanted to contemplate. Before she could stop herself, she said loudly over Kevin's voice. "Yes. A million times yes." She knew it was rude to interrupt his sermon, but wasn't it rude also to make him wait even a moment longer than he had to?

He stopped talking and stared at her. "Are you sure?"

Bridget nodded, her eyes filled with tears. "I couldn't be surer."

He drew a deep breath. "Since my sermon is on the topic of love this morning, I'll briefly explain for those of you who were not at the wedding reception last night. I asked the beautiful woman sitting in the front row to be my wife in front of her entire family and half of the ranch. She told me she had to think about it. She's just given me her answer, and I'm afraid I'm going to have to take a one minute break from my sermon."

Bridget watched him jump down off the stage where his pulpit was and walk to her. He took her hand and drew her to her feet. "No engagement can be official until there's a kiss to seal it." Leaning down he pressed his lips to hers, a sweet kiss filled with promise for the future.

She wrapped her arms around his neck and hugged him close. "I wish I didn't have to go home, but I'll be back by December first." Earlier if she could make it. Of course there was packing to do, and a job to give notice for…and then she'd have to make the drive from Texas. Hopefully there wouldn't be too much snow to drive through, because she'd only driven in snow once or twice in her life.

"We'll talk soon." Jumping back up, he calmly finished his sermon, though no one in the congregation could miss the fact that he couldn't seem to stop grinning, and his eyes tended to be drawn to the woman in the front row, who had given him the words he needed to hear.

After the sermon was over, he accepted the congratulations of everyone there, keeping Bridget's hand firmly in his. Once the church had cleared out, he smiled at her. "You've made me the happiest man alive. I hope you know that." He'd been sweating her answer for too long. Now he knew she'd be his, he couldn't seem to stop grinning.

"What now? Lunch?"

He nodded. "Yeah, let's go to lunch, and we'll talk about our future plans. I don't want to wait long."

She shook her head. "I don't either. I don't much like to be the center of attention, so I'd rather not have a big wedding. Maybe a quiet ceremony as soon as I get back? Is there someone in town who can do it?"

"Sure is." They left the church hand-in-hand to find her parents waiting for them. "Come to lunch with us, so we can make our plans." He wanted her parents to feel like they were gaining a son and not just losing a daughter. It would be different than the family he'd grown up with, because he'd never quite felt like one of the sons there, even though they'd treated him like he was. The seven brothers he'd had all looked like brothers, with their slate gray eyes. His were brown. And he'd never taken their last name. Now he really would belong, because he'd have Bridget by his side forever.

"Absolutely," Mr. Taylor responded. "Glad to get the other one off my hands. I wasn't sure anyone would want her!"

Kevin shook his head. "Of course I want her. She's the most beautiful woman alive. How could I not?"

Together they walked to the restaurant there on the ranch, laughing as people left their tables to congratulate them over and over. Word spread fast in a small town. "I wish I'd brought your ring with me this morning, but I didn't think I'd get an answer in the middle of my sermon." He had to tease her about the moment she'd chosen to respond to his proposal. Hopefully she wouldn't make a habit of interrupting him.

"I didn't think you would either." Bridget shrugged. "It just happened, and I had to share my decision with you."

After lunch, where they decided to marry in a quiet ceremony as soon as she came back to Idaho, Kevin took Bridget for a walk through the new snow. "What made you decide?" he asked.

She shrugged. "I'm not sure. I guess part of it was the way you were so casual about your sermon today. It made me feel like I could be your wife."

"I'm so glad it did." He stopped by the lake and turned to her, taking her hands in his. "I can't tell you how happy you've made me. You may not be the traditional pastor's wife that other men are looking for, but you'll be the right wife for me. That's what matters."

Bridget smiled. "And I know you'll be the right husband for me, but that was never in question. You're practically perfect in every way. Kind of like Mary Poppins."

He groaned. "Another Disney movie? I'm going to spend the rest of my life living on Disney dreams, aren't I?"

"You are. But you'll love every second of it." Bridget grinned at him, loving his mock tortured expression.

"We don't have to go to Disney for our honeymoon, do we?"

She shook her head. "Not if you're willing to wear the Mickey and Minnie groom and bride mouse ears."

"I—Do those really exist?" He said a silent prayer that she was making it up, because he knew he'd agree to whatever she wanted where the wedding was concerned.

"Yup. So how 'bout it? Disney wedding or Disney honeymoon?"

"Wedding, I guess. I'd rather honeymoon in one of the cabins up in the mountains…away from the world. I don't know that I'll ever be ready to share you."

"Just so you can keep being my Prince Charming."

He kissed her forehead. "As long as you're always my Cinderella."

I hope you enjoyed this latest book in the River's End Ranch series. If you'd like to see what Kirsten is up to and sign up for her newsletter, feel free to click here. Curious about the next book in the series by Pamela Kelly? There's an excerpt coming right up!

Chapter Eleven

"YOU JUST MISSED a call from Ahn-dray-uh. She requested that you call her back as soon as possible!" Bernie was half-laughing as Lily walked over and handed her an iced coffee. Every day around 2 p.m., Lily took a mid-afternoon walk to stretch her legs and get a coffee. She sat down at her desk and took a sip of her own hot, black coffee as she gazed out the window.

The sun was shining and it was a gorgeous day at the ranch. Ninety-five percent of the time, Lily loved her job as an event coordinator at River's End Ranch. She planned everything from weddings to corporate dinners, showers, and birthday or anniversary parties. But every once in a while, she had a client that was almost impossible to please, difficult and demanding. Like Andrea Thomas.

"Did she say what she wanted?" Lily asked. She and Bernie shared an office. Bernie was Wade Weston's executive assistant. Wade was one of the six Weston siblings who owned and ran the ranch along with their parents, but they were semi-retired and traveling the country in an RV, so Wade, as general manager, was the main business contact for the ranch. Bernie was an ideal office mate. She was fiercely loyal to Wade and great at her job, but had a sense of humor and was fun to work with. They always covered for each other if one was out of the office.

"I think she may want to change up the menu. Again."

Lily shook her head, and then dialed Andrea's number. Better to just get the call over with. Andrea picked up on the first ring.

"Andrea Thomas, how can I help you?"

"It's Lily Donahue. I had a message that you called?"

"Yes, Lily. We need to go over the menu. I don't think this is going to work." Her tone was crisp and dismissive.

Lily took a breath. "Okay, what did you have in mind?"

For the next twenty minutes, she tried to keep up as Andrea went through all the menu items that needed changing. When she finally hung up the phone, Bernie laughed out loud.

"Are you serious? What could possibly need that much changing?"

"Oh, just about everything. This is an entirely new menu now. One person has a dairy allergy, someone else needs gluten-free and so of course that means we must have two cakes. One chocolate and one that is lemon-raspberry—dairy and gluten-free, of course."

"Of course."

"I wouldn't mind so much if she was just a little nicer about it." Andrea sounded like an angry governess, cold and demanding. Yet she was actually very pretty, blonde and delicate looking, and about Lily's age, but Lily had never met anyone quite like her. It was a disconcerting combination.

"And you still haven't talked to Cody Jamison yet? Even though it's his party?" Bernie asked. Andrea was Cody's executive assistant and to her credit, she was certainly efficient.

"No, though I imagine I'll at least meet him at the party. After all, it is for his parents."

"That's true. I asked Wade about him, and he said they were friends in college, but he hasn't seen him much in recent years. They're both so busy." She was quiet for a moment, then a gleam came into her eye as she added, "He said Cody is single, though, and successful. In addition to running one of the biggest cattle ranches in the area, he and his brother Ben have been doing some real estate investing, buying properties and fixing them up."

Lily made a face. "He doesn't sound my type at all. I wouldn't have anything in common with a businessman."

"Well, he's a cowboy, too. That's kind of romantic."

"You think so? You can have him, then." Lily grinned. "Besides, if he's anything like Andrea, I won't mind if I never meet him."

* * *

Lily kicked off her shoes as soon as she walked through the front door of her condo that night. She hadn't been there long, just six months and it was a rental, but it was exactly the type of place she would love to own one day. The location was ideal, just off Main Street in downtown Riston, which was convenient. It was a short drive to the ranch but also an easy walk to most of the restaurants and bars along Main Street where Lily sometimes moonlighted singing in a little band with her brother, Tyler, and his friend, Mark. Lily did most of the vocals and wrote all of the original songs that they sang. But mostly they did covers of popular country and soft rock music.

"Meow!" Lily reached down and scooped up the small

cat that was loudly demanding her dinner. Hope was a shelter kitty, a pretty, short-haired, seven-year-old girl that had been with Lily since she was two. She had all white paws, a mix of brown and black patches all over and pale green eyes. She was beautiful and tiny. Hope purred and rubbed her head against Lily's chin once or twice, before she'd had enough and wiggled to get down. Lily fed her and then made her way into the living room and opened the windows to let in some fresh air.

She grabbed her guitar, settled on her well-worn living room sofa and started to strum a few chords. This was her favorite time of day. As much as she enjoyed both her job and playing in the band, it was this, creating the music, that was her passion. It relaxed and energized her at the same time.

Lily had an end unit and she was especially thrilled that she could make as much noise as she wanted to now that her neighbors had moved out. She knew it was just a matter of time before someone else moved in, but for now it was nice to not have to worry about bothering anyone. Tyler and Mark were coming over and they were going to be rehearsing one of her new songs. Normally, they did their practicing at Mark's house but his roommate was having people over and this weekend they had a gig booked and wanted to get another practice in. Two hours later, they were just about through their set and were going through Lily's new song for a final time when there was a knock on the door. They stopped playing and both Tyler and Mark looked her way.

"You expecting someone?" Tyler asked.

"No, I have no idea who that is."

She walked to the door, opened it, and took a step back. Standing there was a man who simply took her breath away. He was over six feet tall and lean, with tousled light brown hair and a five o'clock shadow. He was dressed casually, in faded jeans and a gray U of Idaho t-shirt. Lily was about to smile and say hello when he took her by surprise by frowning and saying in an irritated tone, "Do you guys mind keeping it down?" Before she could even reply, he followed it up with, "Do you do this often?"

Lily felt suddenly flustered. He made her nervous. "Um, no. We don't, but we didn't think anyone was next door yet. We're just about done here." Was this her new neighbor? It wasn't the first of the month yet, and they'd only just moved out that morning. "Who are you?" she added.

"I'm Cody Jamison. My brother and I recently bought this building and I guess, for the next month or so, I'll be your new neighbor."

The Cody Jamison? Lily wasn't sure how she felt about that.

"You're going to be living here?" she asked.

"Just initially, while we do some renovating. I don't think it will take long to rent."

"No, I'm sure it won't. I'm Lily. Lily Donahue."

His eyes flickered as if her name sounded familiar.

"I've actually been working with your assistant, Andrea, to plan your parents fiftieth wedding anniversary. I'm the event coordinator at River's End Ranch."

His expression softened at the mention of his parents' party.

"I thought your name sounded familiar." He looked as though he was going to say something else, but Lily quickly jumped in.

"I'm really sorry for the noise. We're done for the night. It won't happen again," she assured him.

He looked at her for a long moment before saying in a curt tone, "Good. I'll be on my way, then. Good night."

He turned to leave and Lily shut the door behind him. Her brother and Mark were already packing up their stuff.

"Jeez, not the friendliest guy. Sorry you have to live next to him," her brother said.

"Hopefully it won't be for too long," Mark added.

"Right," she agreed, realizing that what she'd said earlier to Bernie was so true. Cody Jamison was hot, she'd give him that, but he was most definitely not her type.

About the Author

www.kirstenandmorganna.com

Also by Kirsten Osbourne

To sign up for Kirsten Osbourne's mailing list and receive notice of new titles as they are available text 'BOB' to 42828

For a complete list of books in series order, written by Kirsten, please click here.

CPSIA information can be obtained
at www.ICGtesting.com
Printed in the USA
BVHW080853171119
564073BV00019B/1160/P